W9-CPL-516

The Random House Book of
1001
Questions and Answers About
THE HUMAN BODY

Trevor Day

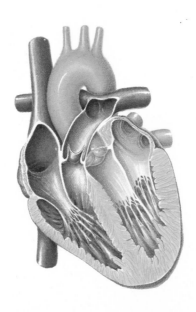

Random House New York

APR. 1996

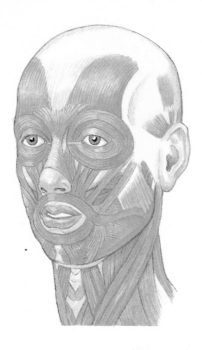

Acknowledgments
The author would like to thank the following people for
their help in researching this book: Claire Tadman, Ali Cass
and the pupils of Year 6, Oakfield Middle School, Frome,
Somerset, Dr. Geoffrey Goats of the University of East
Anglia, Department of Physiotherapy, Angela Bradding of
Colchester Sixth Form College, Fionnuala Strong and
Brendan McLoughlin of Frome, Somerset.

Copyright © 1994 by Grisewood & Dempsey Limited.
All rights reserved under International and Pan-American Copyright
Conventions. Published in the United States by Random House, Inc.,
New York. Originally published in Great Britain by Kingfisher Books
Limited, a Grisewood & Dempsey Company, in 1994.

Library of Congress Cataloging-in-Publication Data
Day, Trevor.
The Random House book of 1001 questions and answers about the
human body / Trevor Day.
    p.   cm.
Simultaneously published in England under title: The human body, in
series: 1001 questions & answers.
    Includes index.
    ISBN 0-679-85432-0
    1. Human physiology—Miscellanea—Juvenile literature. 2. Body,
Human—Miscellanea—Juvenile literature. [1. Body, Human—
Miscellanea. 2. Questions and answers.] I. Title. II. Title: Random
House book of one thousand and one questions and answers about the
human body.
    QP37.D34   1994
    512—dc20   93-6386

Manufactured in Italy 10 9 8 7 6 5 4 3 2

CONTENTS

Body Basics   4

Skeleton and Movement   8

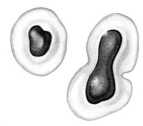
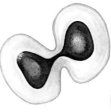

Lungs and Heart   18

Food and Waste   34

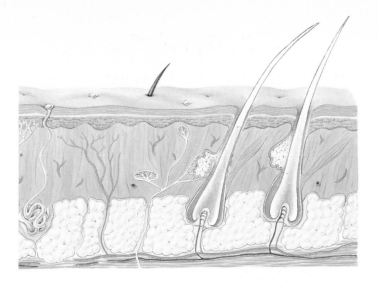

BODY BASICS

What is the human body made of?

About two-thirds of the human body is water. The remaining third is a complicated mixture of chemicals. The water-and-chemical mix is arranged into structures called cells. These are tiny, but you can see them using a microscope.

What is a cell?

Cells are the small building blocks of the body. They have a very thin outer layer, called the cell membrane, which lets in food and oxygen and lets out waste. Much of the cell is a jellylike substance called cytoplasm. Activity inside the cell is controlled by the nucleus.

How many cells are in our bodies?

There are billions and billions of cells in the human body.

What happens inside a cell?

Within the cytoplasm are tiny structures called organelles. Each organelle has a different job to do. For example, materials for growth and repair (proteins) are made on tiny round grains called ribosomes. These are found along a folded membrane called the endoplasmic reticulum. Round organelles called lysosomes contain chemicals that break down harmful substances or worn-out parts of the cell that need to be replaced.

What is the nucleus?

The nucleus is an organelle that functions as the cell's "brain." Inside the nucleus are 46 tangled threads called chromosomes. Each chromosome carries instructions for the jobs done by other organelles inside the cell's body.

What are mitochondria?

Mitochondria are the tiny, rod-shaped power-houses found in every cell of the body. They use oxygen to break down food and release energy so the other structures in the cell can carry out their jobs.

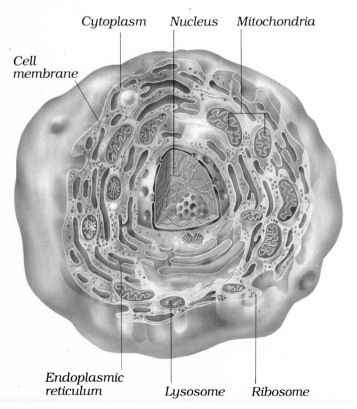

Cytoplasm   Nucleus   Mitochondria

Cell membrane

Endoplasmic reticulum   Lysosome   Ribosome

The body's cells contain a number of different, specialized organelles. These organelles carry out the chemical processes necessary for the body to work smoothly.

How long do cells live?

Some cells live for only a few days—others last for years. Some of the cells lining our intestines live for as little as one or two days, while bone cells last for 15 to 20 years. In most cases, dead cells are replaced by new ones. However, nerve cells cannot be replaced.

Do all cells look the same?

Although all cells have things in common, they do not all look the same. In fact, there are several hundred different kinds of cells in the body. Their shape and size relate to the job they do. Nerve cells are long and thin, to carry messages from one part of the body to another. Cells lining the inside of the mouth are round and flat, and are pressed against one another to form a protective layer.

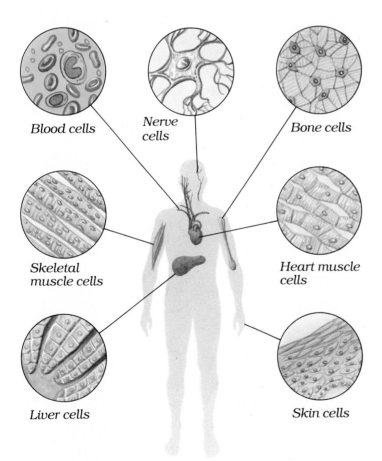

Blood cells

Nerve cells

Bone cells

Skeletal muscle cells

Heart muscle cells

Liver cells

Skin cells

Human cells vary to suit their different functions. Nerve cells are long and thin, while bone cells are densely packed.

Why do cells split themselves in two?

Cells split in two when they have reached their maximum size and cannot grow any larger. Much of the body's growth takes place this way.

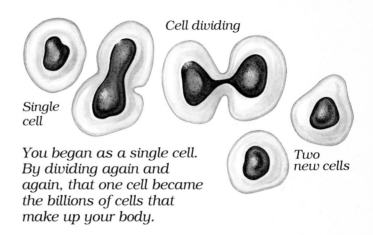

Cell dividing

Single cell

Two new cells

You began as a single cell. By dividing again and again, that one cell became the billions of cells that make up your body.

Which is the largest cell?

The largest human cell is the egg cell, found in women. It is about 0.008 inch across, a little smaller than the period at the end of this sentence. The longest cells are the nerve cells in your legs. Although they are very thin, they are up to 39 inches long. They carry messages from your feet to your spine and back again.

How small is the smallest cell?

Among the smallest cells are red blood cells, which are less than 0.0004 inch across. Sperm cells, found in men, are also very small. The head of the sperm is about 0.0002 inch across.

What do cells need to stay alive?

Cells need three basic things to stay alive: food, oxygen, and a "friendly," watery environment with a careful balance of the right chemicals, so that the cell can carry out its tasks properly. The cell can propel its waste into this watery environment, too.

How do cells get food?

Food and oxygen are carried to the cells by blood, which also takes away waste. Blood provides the tissue fluid in which cells live, too.

What are the body fluids?

The four main body fluids are blood, lymph, tissue fluid, and the fluid inside cells. An adult contains 32 to 42 quarts of water, but only 4 to 5 quarts of this is in the blood. Most of the fluid in our body is found inside the cells and as tissue fluid surrounding the cells. Some of the tissue fluid drains away and forms lymph in a system of tubes called lymph vessels.

What are tissues?

Any collection of cells of the same type, working together to do a particular job, is a tissue. Most cells in the body are grouped together in this way to form different types of tissue.

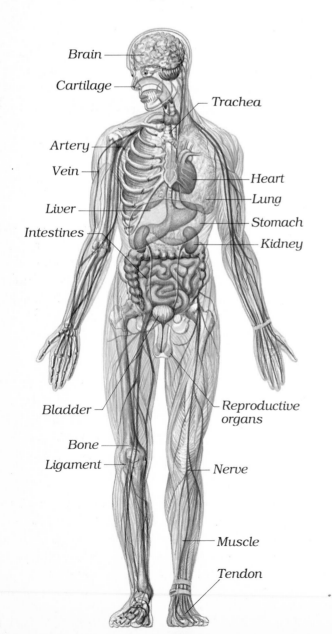

Brain
Cartilage
Trachea
Artery
Vein
Heart
Lung
Liver
Stomach
Intestines
Kidney
Bladder
Reproductive organs
Bone
Ligament
Nerve
Muscle
Tendon

How many types of tissue are there?

There are dozens of types of tissue, but most can be put into one of four categories. Lining, or epithelial, tissue covers the outer and inner surfaces of the body. Connective tissue links parts of the body together and holds them in place. Bone is a type of connective tissue. Muscle tissue and nervous tissue such as that found in the brain are the two other main types.

What is an organ?

An organ is a structure made of different tissues collected together to do a particular job. For example, the heart contains lining tissue, nervous tissue, and muscles, all held together by connective tissue. These tissues work together to pump blood around the body. The eye, the brain, the heart, and the liver are all organs.

What is an organ system?

An organ usually does not work on its own; instead several organs work together as an organ system. For example, the stomach, liver, and pancreas work together as an organ system to process the food we have eaten and break it down into useful substances.

How many organ systems do we have?

We have nine organ systems in all. The skeletal and muscular systems support, protect, and move parts of the body. The nervous system and endocrine system coordinate the body's actions. The circulatory (transport) system carries blood around the body. The respiratory system is responsible for breathing. Food is broken down by the digestive system, the urinary system removes waste from the body, and the reproductive system produces children.

Groups of organs working together to perform specialized jobs are called organ systems. There are nine systems in all, carrying out tasks such as supporting the body (the skeletal and muscular systems), breaking down food (the digestive system), or creating a new life (the reproductive system).

What is a gland?

A gland is a structure that produces a fluid the body needs to work properly. An entire organ, such as the liver, can be a gland. Or glands can be much smaller, like the tiny glands in the skin that produce sweat, and the glands that empty into the mouth and produce saliva.

Where are your extremities?

Your extremities are your arms and hands, and your legs and feet.

What are membranes?

Membranes are extremely thin layers of tissue that cover surfaces or line cavities inside the body.

What is mucus?

Mucus is the name of the sticky, slippery fluid produced by glands in certain membranes. Mucus is produced inside the mouth and the rest of the digestive tract, and in the air passages leading to the lungs. It protects these delicate surfaces from damage.

Your metabolism speeds up when you are active, so that the cells can produce the extra energy your body needs. This chart shows how much energy you use during different activities.

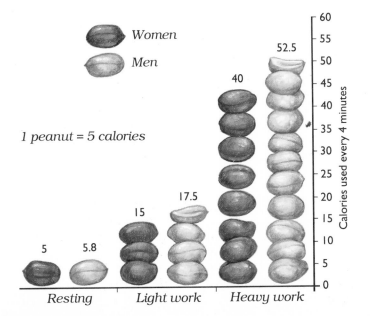

1 peanut = 5 calories

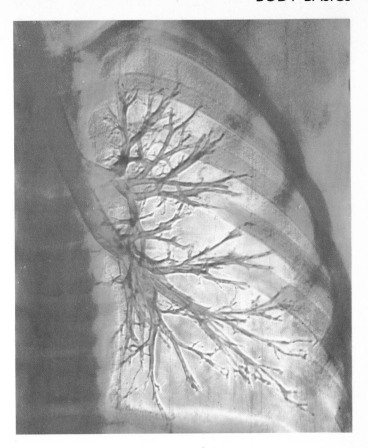

This false-color X ray shows the major blood vessels in the lung.

How is the body studied?

Probes and scanners can be used to "see" inside the body without having to cut into it. X rays, ultrasound (high-frequency sound waves), and radioactive tracers are among the techniques used. Tissue samples can also be examined by magnifying cells under a microscope.

What is your metabolism?

Metabolism is a general term that covers all the activity inside your body, such as the chemical reactions that take place in the cells to produce energy or materials for growth and repair.

What are enzymes?

Enzymes are special proteins that speed up chemical reactions inside your body. There are hundreds of different enzymes. The best-known are the digestive enzymes, which work inside your stomach and intestines to break down food.

SKELETON and MOVEMENT

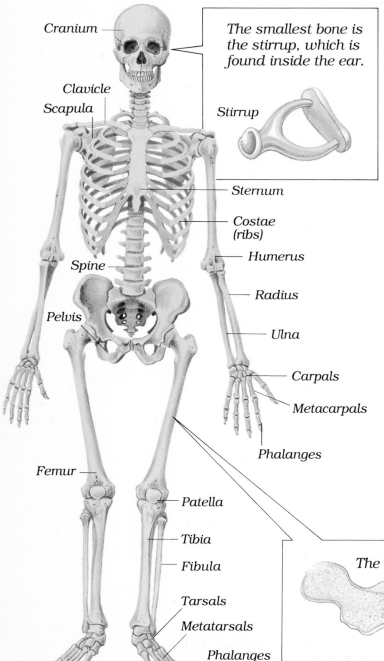

Cranium

The smallest bone is the stirrup, which is found inside the ear.

Stirrup

Clavicle

Scapula

Sternum

Costae (ribs)

Humerus

Spine

Radius

Pelvis

Ulna

Carpals

Metacarpals

Phalanges

Femur

Patella

Tibia

Fibula

Tarsals

Metatarsals

Phalanges

How many bones are there in the body?

Adults have about 206 bones. The number may vary slightly from person to person because some people have an extra pair of ribs, and some have more bones in their hands and feet.

What do bones do?

Bones support the soft parts of our body. Without bones, we would be a messy blob. Bones also protect vital organs in our body from physical damage. For example, the skull protects our brain and eyes, and our rib cage protects the lungs and heart. Our skeleton also acts as a system of levers against which muscles can pull. This allows us to move. Finally, some bones make blood cells.

Which is the smallest bone?

In the middle ear there is a tiny bone called the stirrup, or stapes. It is only 0.12 inch long and weighs about 0.0001 ounce.

Which is the largest bone?

The largest bone is the thigh bone, or femur. Its special design means it is also the strongest bone. A man who is 6 feet tall will have a femur about one and a half feet long.

The thigh bone, or femur, is the longest bone.

Femur

8

How many different types of bone are there?

Bones are grouped according to their shape. There are four different kinds. Long bones are found in the arms, hands, legs, and feet. Short bones make up the wrists and ankles. The ribs, breastbone, and bones of the skull (cranium) are flat bones, while bones of the spine and face are irregular in shape.

How much do my bones weigh?

Bones weigh surprisingly little. Living bone consists of roughly equal amounts of water and solid material. Bone makes up about 12 percent of your body weight. The bones of a person who weighs 110 pounds would weigh a little more than 13 pounds.

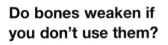

In space, bones no longer have to combat the force of gravity, so they grow more slowly and lose weight.

Do bones weaken if you don't use them?

Yes. Bones respond to the stresses and strains of movement by growing and reinforcing themselves. If they are not used they will lose weight. In the weightlessness of space, the Apollo astronauts lost 0.14 ounce of bone in a month.

Are bones living or dead?

Bones are alive. Bone contains thousands of living bone cells. The cells produce a mixture of nonliving salts that give bones their strength. Like other living cells, the bone cells have a blood supply to bring them food and oxygen and to remove waste.

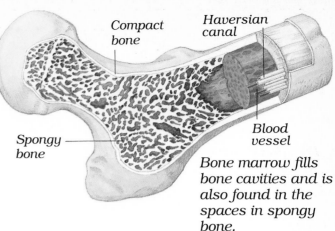

Compact bone — *Haversian canal* — *Blood vessel* — *Spongy bone*

Bone marrow fills bone cavities and is also found in the spaces in spongy bone.

What is inside a bone?

The outer layer of bone is called compact bone. It is hard and very strong. The inner layer of bone has lots of spaces, and so is called spongy bone. This bone is also strong but is fairly light, so it keeps down the overall weight of the skeleton and makes it easy for us to move. In the middle of bone there is a cavity filled with a substance called bone marrow.

What is bone marrow?

Bone marrow is a jellylike fatty tissue found in the hollow spaces in spongy bone and in the cavity in the middle of long bones. It manufactures up to 5 billion red blood cells each day, as well as making certain types of white blood cells. It is also a fat store.

Do blood vessels run through bones?

Yes. In the outer layer of bone the cells form rings around narrow spaces called Haversian canals. Each of these canals has a blood vessel running through it.

Do bones have a skin?

Yes. All bones are surrounded by a thin skin, or membrane, called the periosteum. The periosteum contains specialized cells, called osteoblasts, which make new bone cells.

How strong is bone?

For its weight, bone is as strong as steel and four times stronger than the same amount of reinforced concrete.

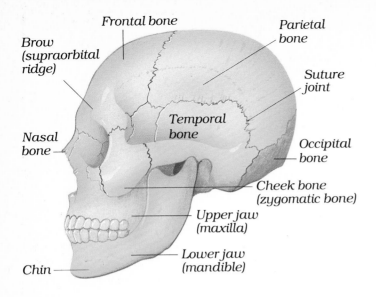

Most of the bones in the skull are knitted together to provide a protective casing for the brain.

How many bones make up the skull?

Although you might think that the skull is a single bone, it is actually made up of 29 different bones. This total includes all the bones in your face, plus the three small bones in each ear. Most of the bones in your skull are knitted together by immovable joints called sutures. The only bones that move freely are the jaw bone and the bones of the middle ear.

What makes bone so strong?

The hard part of bone is made up mainly of the mineral calcium phosphate. Through this run fibers of a protein called collagen. Calcium phosphate gives bone its strength and collagen gives bone its bendiness. See this for yourself. If you boil a chicken bone, the collagen is removed and the bone becomes brittle. If a chicken bone is put in strong vinegar, the calcium dissolves and makes the bone bendy, like rubber.

A plaster cast holds the ends of a broken bone together while the bone cells multiply to heal the break.

What is my patella?

The patella is the technical name for your knee-cap. It gets its name from the limpet, whose Latin name is *patella*. A kneecap looks somewhat like the shape of the limpet's shell. The patella is in a tendon at the front of the knee.

How do broken bones mend?

When a bone is broken, bone cells in the damaged region grow and multiply. They spread through the damaged region to close up the breaks. If the two broken ends of the bone are lined up and held still inside a plaster cast, the bone will heal. In children and young adults, this healing process takes 12 weeks or less for bones in the arm or leg.

Which bones are most commonly broken?

The forearm bones, the ulna and radius, are broken more often than any others.

What is a simple fracture?

A simple fracture occurs when a bone breaks cleanly in two. If there is more than one break in a bone the fracture is compound. If the broken ends of the bone tear into blood vessels or nerves, the break is called a complicated fracture.

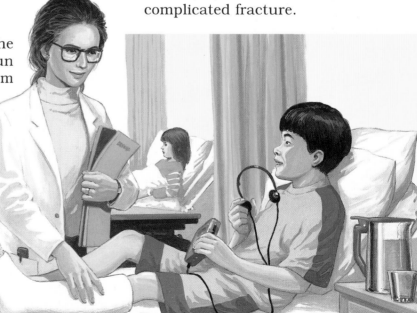

Where are the vertebrae?

The vertebrae (just one is a vertebra) are the bones that make up the spine. There are 33 altogether, linked in a flexible chain that runs from the neck to the lower back (the bottom nine vertebrae are fused together). The top two vertebrae, the atlas and axis vertebrae, have a different structure than the others. This means they can work as a pair to allow the head to nod and turn freely.

What are ribs for?

The ribs form a protective cage around the heart and lungs. You can feel your rib cage extending from the flat bone in the middle of your chest, right around your sides to your backbone. The ribs also swing up and down when you breathe to inflate and deflate your lungs.

How do bones grow?

In a fetus (unborn baby) the bones are made of cartilage. By the time the baby is born, most of the cartilage has turned to bone. This process is called ossification. But growth areas still remain near the ends of the bone. This is where new bone cells are formed. These growth areas disappear when the skeleton reaches full size. Even then, the bone can still alter its shape slightly and repair itself when it is broken or damaged.

Do I have a wishbone?

Not quite. The wishbone of a bird is formed from the two collarbones, which are fused together for strength. When you bend a wishbone, one of the collarbones breaks. We have collarbones too, but they are separate, not fused together, so they do not form a wishbone.

What is my funny bone?

Your funny bone isn't really a bone at all. It is the spot in your elbow where your humerus, the long arm bone near your shoulder, meets your ulnar nerve. When you bump the back of your elbow, the nerve tingles all the way down into your hand.

Atlas vertebra

Axis vertebra

The atlas vertebra twists on the axis vertebra, allowing you to turn your head from side to side.

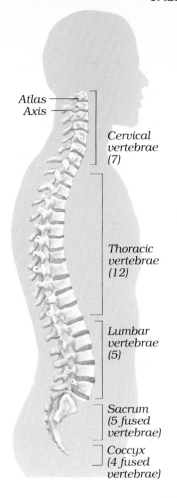

Atlas
Axis
Cervical vertebrae (7)
Thoracic vertebrae (12)
Lumbar vertebrae (5)
Sacrum (5 fused vertebrae)
Coccyx (4 fused vertebrae)

The backbone, or spine, is a linked chain of small bones called vertebrae. Each vertebra can move only a little, but the chain of small movements adds up to make the spine very flexible.

Do I write with my phalanges?

The phalanges are the bones in your fingers, thumbs, and toes. Obviously, you only use some of your phalanges when you write.

Why do people shrink as they grow old?

As people get older, the cartilage pads that protect the bones of the spine become thinner. This leads to height loss. Because people's muscles become weaker with age, their posture changes. This also makes them look smaller.

Do bones get brittle as we get older?

Bones are probably strongest when we are in our late twenties. Many people over 60, women in particular, suffer from a condition called osteoporosis. The bones lose some calcium and become more brittle. In women who suffer very badly, the process can sometimes be halted or slowed by medication.

Joints

What is a joint?

A joint is a place where two or more bones meet. A joint may be fixed (like the skull), or movable (the knee). Because we have a jointed skeleton, we are able to make many twisting, turning movements—even though our bones cannot bend.

What keeps bones from coming apart at joints?

Strong, elastic straps of tissue called ligaments hold bones together at joints.

What is cartilage?

Cartilage is a slippery blue or white substance found at the ends of bones. It allows bones to move against one another without causing damage. Cartilage is more slippery than ice.

Are our joints lubricated?

Yes, some are. At joints that are used often, a liquid called synovial fluid is sandwiched between the bones. The fluid acts as a lubricant to further reduce friction and rubbing between one bone and the other.

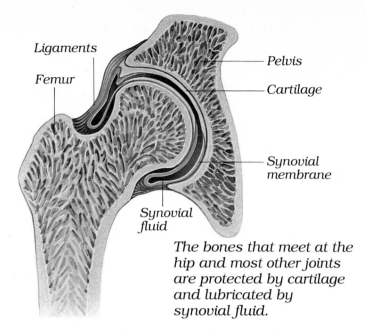

The bones that meet at the hip and most other joints are protected by cartilage and lubricated by synovial fluid.

How does cartilage act as a shock absorber?

Cartilage is flexible and gives when bones are jarred, so it makes a good shock absorber. The cartilage disks in between the vertebrae in the neck and back have a cushioning effect that protects the spine from damage.

How many joints do we have?

We have over one hundred joints altogether. There are four main types. Ball-and-socket joints are found at the hip and shoulder. They give free movement in many directions. Hinge joints, such as those at the knee and elbow, allow movement in only one direction, rather like a door hinge. Suture joints join together bones in the skull and pelvis. These joints are rigid. Swivel joints, which are found in between vertebrae in the spine, allow small tilting and turning movements.

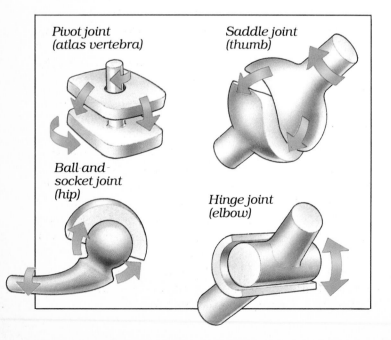

Joints make it easy to move the skeleton. Some of the most common types are shown at left. The joint between our thumb and fingers allows us to handle objects with precision (right).

Do double-jointed people really have extra joints?

No. They have the same number of joints as everyone else. When we describe people as double-jointed, we mean that they can bend their limbs further than most people, sometimes in unusual directions. They can do this because their ligaments are very loose.

Why do joints sometimes "crack"?

Sometimes, when you suddenly bend a joint at your elbow or knee, it makes a cracking sound. Nobody really knows why this happens. One possibility is that tiny air bubbles suddenly form in the joint. These sounds might also be made by taut tendons and ligaments as they snap over bone when you move a joint. Cracking joints continually out of habit can start to damage the joint surface.

What is a dislocation?

When a bone comes out of place at a joint, and the ligaments that hold the joint together are stretched or torn, the joint is dislocated. The dislocated bone must be helped back into place, and the joint rested, if the ligaments are to heal. There is also damage to other tissues in the joint. Dislocations of very flexible joints, such as the shoulder, are most common.

How do you sprain a joint?

If a joint is twisted too far, the ligaments may tear. This is how the joint at your ankle or wrist becomes sprained.

What is special about our thumb joint?

Many animals have five fingers on each hand, but having four fingers and a thumb is a feature special to humans and some apes. Our thumb is called an "opposable" thumb. This means that, because of the joint between the thumb and hand, the thumb can swing around and work in the opposite direction to the four fingers. Our thumb can work with each of our fingertips. It is this action that allows us to handle objects so delicately and with precision.

This circus contortionist is extraordinarily supple because she has very loose ligaments.

How do people "slip a disk"?

Between each vertebra in the spine is a pad, or disk, of cartilage. If the back is strained, this disk may burst, and part of it will press against the spinal cord or one of the spinal nerves. If it presses against a nerve in your spine it can cause a tremendous amount of pain.

Why does the knee have extra cartilage?

The knee joint is under a lot of stress, so it has two extra pieces of cartilage to strengthen and protect it. If these tear, pieces may lodge between the bones and the joint may lock. An operation is usually needed to remove the damaged piece of cartilage.

What is arthritis?

Arthritis is a disease of the joints. In rheumatoid arthritis, the region of the joint that produces synovial fluid is attacked by the body's own defenses. Without the fluid, the heads of the bones wear more quickly, and the bones may even stick together. Another form of arthritis, called osteoarthritis, is more common among athletes. Wear on the joint causes the bone ends to erode faster than they are repaired and movement becomes very painful.

Muscles

How do muscles help us move?

Joints allow the skeleton to move, but muscles produce the movement by pulling the bone into a new position.

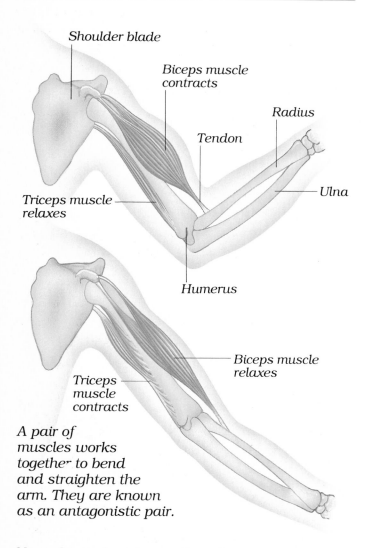

Shoulder blade

Biceps muscle contracts

Radius

Tendon

Triceps muscle relaxes

Ulna

Humerus

Biceps muscle relaxes

Triceps muscle contracts

A pair of muscles works together to bend and straighten the arm. They are known as an antagonistic pair.

How do we bend our elbow?

The biceps muscle is attached to your shoulder blade at one end and to a bone in the forearm at the other. The triceps muscle is also connected to the shoulder blade and forearm. When the biceps contracts (shortens), the triceps is relaxed (lengthens) and the elbow bends. When the triceps contracts and the biceps is relaxed, the elbow joint straightens.

Why do most muscles work in pairs?

Muscles can only pull, or contract; they cannot push. Either another muscle, or gravity, must pull a muscle out into a longer shape when it is relaxed. That is why most muscles come in pairs and work against each other. We call such muscles antagonistic pairs.

How are muscles attached to bone?

Muscles are attached to bone by tendons. These are strings of a tough protein called collagen. You can see the tendons in your wrist if you clench your fist.

Where are muscles found?

There are muscles all over your body—not just in places where there are bones to move. The heart and stomach, for example, both contain muscle.

What is muscle tone?

Muscles are usually neither fully contracted nor fully relaxed, but are partly contracted to help support your body and hold it in position. This is muscle tone. The fibers in each muscle contract in turn, so they do not get too tired.

How much do my muscles weigh?

Your muscles make up about 40 percent of your overall weight. In all, they weigh much more than your bones.

How many muscles do you have?

You have about 650 muscles, with over 50 in your face alone. You use 17 muscles to smile, but over 40 to frown.

Which is the largest muscle?

This is the gluteus maximus, the muscle that runs from the buttock to the back of the thigh. However, in women, one muscle may show a dramatic increase in size. During pregnancy, the uterus (womb) increases in weight from just over an ounce to more than 2 pounds. That's over thirty times larger.

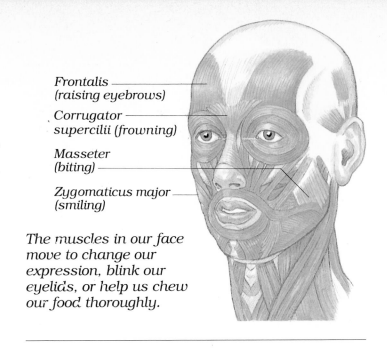

Frontalis
(raising eyebrows)

Corrugator
supercilii (frowning)

Masseter
(biting)

Zygomaticus major
(smiling)

The muscles in our face move to change our expression, blink our eyelids, or help us chew our food thoroughly.

Which is the strongest muscle?

Size for size, the strongest muscle in your body is the masseter. One masseter is located on each side of the mouth. Working together, the masseters give a biting force of about 150 pounds.

Which is the longest muscle?

The longest muscle is the sartorius, which runs from the pelvis and across the front of the thigh to the top of the tibia below the knee. You use the sartorius when you draw your leg into a cross-legged sitting position.

Which is the smallest muscle?

The smallest muscle is the stapedius. It damps down the movement of the stapes (stirrup) bone in the middle ear, preventing damage to the middle and inner ear. The stapedius muscle is less than 0.01 inch long.

Which muscle has the longest name?

The muscle with the longest name is the levator labii superioris alaeque nasi. This muscle runs down your face to your nostril and upper lip. Contracting this muscle gives an "Elvis Presley" lip curl.

Which is the most active muscle?

It has been estimated that the eye muscles move more than 100,000 times a day. Many of these movements take place during dreaming.

How many muscles are there in my hands?

You have more than 30 muscles in each forearm and hand. These are needed to control the delicate movements of the fingers.

Which muscles never rest?

Heart (cardiac) muscle keeps contracting 70 or so times a minute, while the smooth muscle in your digestive tract moves all the time.

The muscles that move our arms, legs, and body are voluntary muscles. These muscles are made to work when we want them to.

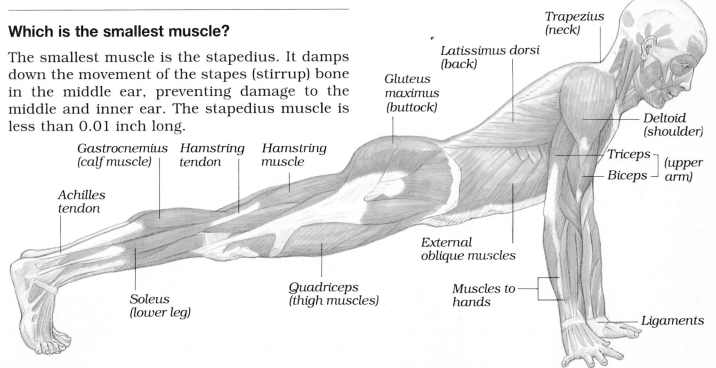

Gastrocnemius
(calf muscle)

Hamstring
tendon

Hamstring
muscle

Achilles
tendon

Soleus
(lower leg)

Quadriceps
(thigh muscles)

External
oblique muscles

Muscles to
hands

Ligaments

Trapezius
(neck)

Latissimus dorsi
(back)

Gluteus
maximus
(buttock)

Deltoid
(shoulder)

Triceps
(upper
arm)

Biceps

15

What are muscles made of?

Muscles are made of thousands of cells called muscle fibers. It is these cells that shorten when a muscle contracts. The cells are bundled together and surrounded by a layer of connective tissue, which holds them in place.

Do all the fibers shorten at once?

No. Only some of the fibers shorten, so the pulling power of the muscle varies. This is particularly useful for delicate movements.

How do muscle fibers shorten?

Each muscle cell contains thin rods that partly overlap. These rods slide past each other to make the muscle fiber shorter.

Is there more than one sort of muscle?

There are three main muscle types: smooth muscle, cardiac muscle, and skeletal muscle.

What are voluntary muscles?

Muscles that we can control by thinking are called voluntary, or skeletal, muscles. Involuntary muscles are the kind that work automatically. Smooth muscle, which moves food along the digestive system, and cardiac muscle, which produces the pumping of the heart, are both involuntary muscles.

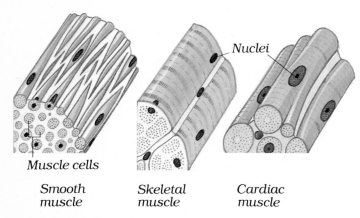

The three types of muscle are made up of different muscle cells. Skeletal muscle cells are the longest, and have several nuclei, while cardiac and smooth muscle cells have only one nucleus.

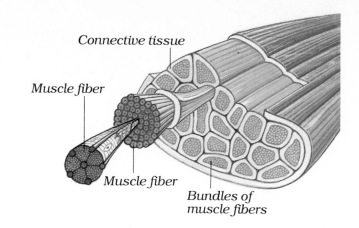

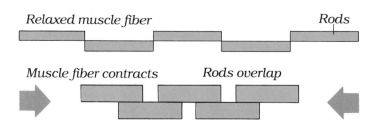

Muscles consist of bundles of fibers. The fibers contain rods, which slide over each other to shorten the fiber when the muscle contracts.

Are muscles different shapes and sizes?

Yes. Most muscles in the arms and legs are long and thin. The diaphragm, which is used for breathing, is a flat sheet of muscle. You also have three flat layers of muscle across your abdomen.

Why do muscles get tired?

When a muscle works very hard, it takes some of the energy it needs by breaking down stored food without using oxygen. This process is called anaerobic respiration. It causes a waste substance called lactic acid to build up inside the muscle, stopping it from working properly.

What causes a cramp?

When too much lactic acid builds up, it causes the muscle to contract strongly and painfully. This is called a cramp. A cramp occurs when you start to exercise a little-used muscle, or if you have been sitting or standing in an uncomfortable position. To deal with a cramp, massage and gently stretch the painful muscle.

What does it mean to be physically fit?

Physical fitness is the ability of your whole body, including the muscles, heart, and lungs, and all other body parts, to work well together. Fitness involves three things: strength (how easily your muscles work); suppleness (being able to move and bend easily); and stamina (being able to keep exercising without tiring quickly).

Exercise is not only good for you, it can be fun as well. You can keep your muscles exercised by taking part in a number of different sports.

What are the benefits of regular exercise?

Exercise helps you look good, feel good, stay healthy, and make the most of your life. It strengthens your muscles and helps maintain good muscle tone. It can alter your body shape and improve your posture. It exercises the heart muscle and helps keep a good blood flow through blood vessels. It can also help relieve stress, create a feeling of well-being, and aid sleep. Quite a list!

Gymnastics

Baseball

Tennis

Basketball

Cycling

Soccer

Why is it important to warm up before vigorous exercise?

Warming up allows your muscles to prepare themselves for exercise. Blood carrying food and oxygen flows into them, and wastes like carbon dioxide are removed. Also, the muscles do actually get warmer. All this helps them to work well when you exercise, and makes them less likely to be pulled, torn, or strained.

How does someone pull a muscle?

A pulled muscle results when a muscle is over-stretched. Some of the muscle fibers actually tear. A pulled muscle feels tight and painful.

How can I strengthen my muscles?

Exercises that involve bending, stretching, tensing, and relaxing are good for strength and suppleness. Weight lifting and exercises such as chin-ups, push-ups, and sit-ups are all good examples.

What is a stitch?

A stitch is a short, sharp pain in the abdomen or side. You sometimes get a stitch during exercise (usually running) if you are not used to it. It is caused by blood being sent to exercising muscles. This starves the abdominal muscles of blood and makes them go into spasm, causing pain.

LUNGS and HEART

What is respiration?

Respiration is the process by which oxygen is used in cells to release energy from food. At the same time, carbon dioxide and water are released as waste products. The word "respiration" can also be used to mean breathing.

How big is an air sac?

An air sac is about 0.008 inch across. The wall of an air sac is a single layer of cells only four-millionths of an inch across. Having such a thin wall helps gases pass easily between the air sac and the capillaries that surround it.

What happens when we breathe in?

When we breathe in, we draw air in through our nose or mouth. The air is mainly nitrogen (79 percent), with about 21 percent oxygen and 0.04 percent carbon dioxide. This mixture of gases travels down the windpipe, or trachea, into two large tubes called bronchi, one leading to each lung. From here the air travels into a system of air passages called bronchioles and finally reaches millions of tiny air sacs, called alveoli, inside each lung.

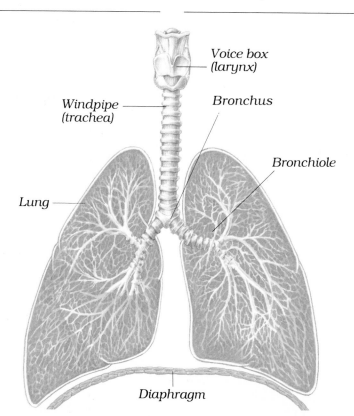

Voice box (larynx)

Windpipe (trachea)

Bronchus

Bronchiole

Lung

Diaphragm

The lungs are the main breathing organs. Inside them, branching air passages lead to millions of tiny air sacs. Here, oxygen from the air is exchanged with waste carbon dioxide from the blood. The oxygen is then carried in the blood to the cells of the body.

What happens inside the air sacs?

Within the air sacs, oxygen is picked up by tiny blood vessels called capillaries and carried to all the body's cells. At the same time, the capillaries release carbon dioxide and water vapor into the air sacs, so that it can be breathed out.

What happens when we breathe out?

When we breathe out, air takes the reverse route from our air sacs to our nose or mouth. But the content of the air is slightly different. The air we breathe out contains less oxygen than before and more carbon dioxide and water vapor.

How do plants give us oxygen?

Plants give out oxygen when they make their food. This process is called photosynthesis. They take in water and carbon dioxide and with the help of sunlight convert these chemicals to oxygen and sugars. By doing this they help maintain the oxygen levels in the air around us. We do not use up all the oxygen in the air because it is constantly replaced by plants.

Why are air sacs so small?

Our lungs need to have a very large surface inside them to be able to do their job: picking up the oxygen we need and getting rid of the carbon dioxide we do not want. Packing the lungs full of tiny air sacs increases the surface area inside the lungs and allows many capillaries into the lungs to collect the oxygen.

How big are our lungs?

Between them our lungs have a surface area of about 84 square yards—bigger than the floor of a squash court.

How many air sacs are in our lungs?

There are about 300 million air sacs in each lung. They are arranged in clusters around the ends of tiny tubes called bronchioles. Each air sac is supplied with several capillaries.

When we breathe in, the diaphragm flattens and the chest cavity expands. Air rushes in to fill our lungs. When we breathe out, the diaphragm relaxes, and air is forced out of the lungs.

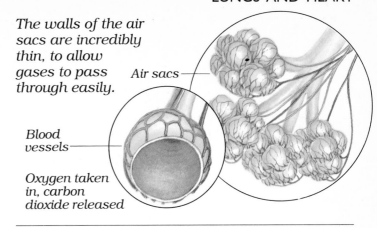

The walls of the air sacs are incredibly thin, to allow gases to pass through easily.

Air sacs

Blood vessels

Oxygen taken in, carbon dioxide released

What is the diaphragm?

The diaphragm is a curved sheet of muscle that separates our chest cavity from our abdomen. The diaphragm and the muscles between the ribs are the main muscles that we use to breathe. When we breathe in, the diaphragm is taut and flattened, and helps increase the size of the chest cavity. When we breathe out, the diaphragm is relaxed, and is domed upward to reduce the size of the chest cavity.

How do our ribs help us breathe in?

Movements of our ribs alter the size of our chest cavity. When we breathe in, our ribs swing upward and outward. This causes our chest cavity to get larger, which lowers the air pressure inside. Air is drawn into the lungs from outside to raise the pressure to normal.

How do we use our ribs to breathe out?

When we breathe out, our ribs swing downward and backward and our chest cavity gets smaller. Air from our lungs is pushed out through our nose and mouth.

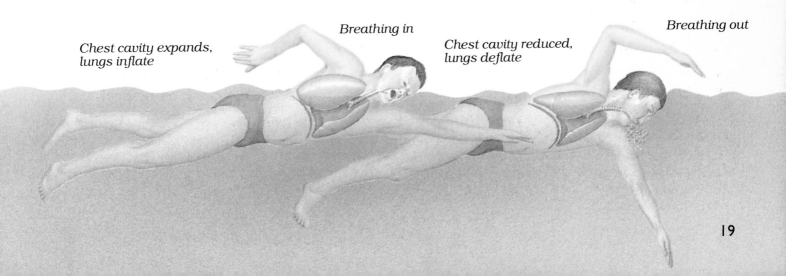

Breathing in

Chest cavity expands, lungs inflate

Breathing out

Chest cavity reduced, lungs deflate

How much air do our lungs hold?

On average, the lungs of an adult man can hold about 6 quarts of air, and those of a woman, about 4.5 quarts.

Do we use all the air in our lungs?

When we are sitting or standing, we breathe in and out only about 10 percent of the air in our lungs. When we exercise, this figure can go up to about 60 percent. About 20 percent of the air in our lungs remains trapped in our air sacs. We cannot get rid of it, no matter how hard we breathe out.

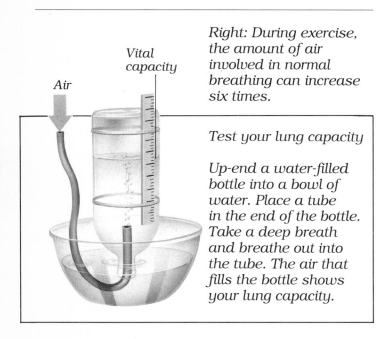

Right: During exercise, the amount of air involved in normal breathing can increase six times.

Test your lung capacity

Up-end a water-filled bottle into a bowl of water. Place a tube in the end of the bottle. Take a deep breath and breathe out into the tube. The air that fills the bottle shows your lung capacity.

What is the vital capacity?

The vital capacity is the maximum amount of air that you can breathe in or out in one breath. The average vital capacity for adult men is about 4.5 quarts, and for women, about 3.5 quarts.

Why do we breathe faster when we exercise?

When we exercise, our muscles do more work and therefore need more energy. They get this energy from food, which is broken down during respiration. Since respiration uses up oxygen, we breathe faster to supply the extra oxygen our muscles need.

Why don't we have to think about breathing?

We don't have to think about breathing because a part of the brain does the job for us. The medulla oblongata—the bulge where the spinal cord joins the brain—contains the control center for breathing. It is an amazingly sensitive chemical detector. During exercise, the level of waste carbon dioxide in the body goes up. The control center senses this and sends signals to the diaphragm and the rib muscles to work harder. We can override the control center if we wish, and change our breathing pattern.

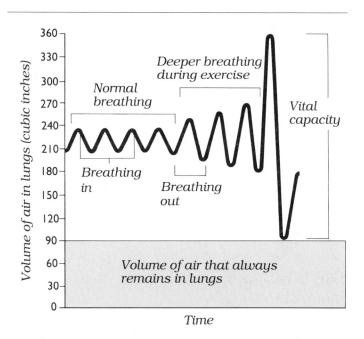

Why is it better to breathe through your nose than your mouth?

Air breathed in through your nose is warmed to a comfortable temperature for your lungs, and moistened and cleaned more effectively than air breathed in through your mouth. Small hairs in the nose filter out dirt. Mucus inside the nose traps some of the dirt, and tiny hairs called cilia push this to the throat, where it is swallowed.

Why aren't our lungs full of dirt?

Like the nose, the air passages in the lungs have mucus and cilia to help clean the air breathed in.

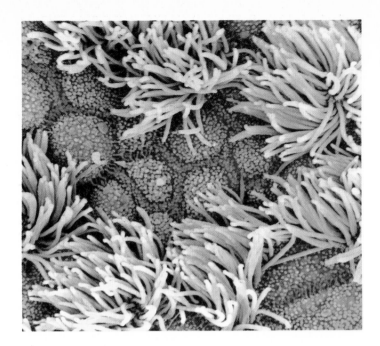

The cilia in the windpipe show as grass-like hairs in this greatly magnified view.

What is the epiglottis?

The epiglottis is a flap of cartilage at the top of the windpipe. It acts as a gateway, stopping food from entering. When you swallow, the epiglottis diverts food down the esophagus, away from the windpipe.

Why is breathing harder on top of a mountain?

The higher up you climb, the thinner the air becomes. This means that with each breath you are taking in much less oxygen than you would normally. Breathing is therefore more difficult on a high mountain. Exercise also becomes difficult because you have to breathe much more heavily to get the oxygen you need.

Why do some athletes train at high altitude?

Long-distance events, such as marathons and 5,000-meter races, rely heavily on athletes' ability to carry oxygen to their muscles. By training at high altitude—and becoming used to thin air—athletes improve their blood's ability to carry oxygen. This improves their athletic performance even if they are competing in races at sea level.

Can astronauts breathe on the moon?

Without special breathing equipment, astronauts would not be able to breathe on the moon. This is because the moon has no atmosphere. So astronauts must take their own supply of oxygen into space.

Can people breathe underwater?

People can breathe underwater if they take their own air supply with them. Divers strap metal tanks of compressed air onto their backs before diving below the surface, and breathe from the tank through special equipment.

How can a diver's lungs burst?

As a diver rises to the surface of the water, the compressed air in his lungs expands. If he does not breathe out at a steady rate, his lungs could become overfilled and burst. All divers learn how to breathe out when they are rising through the water.

Could a diver breathe pure oxygen?

Believe it or not, you can have too much of a good thing. Pure oxygen at high pressure is a poison, and can cause seizures or even death.

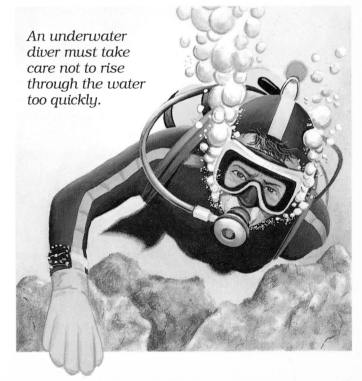

An underwater diver must take care not to rise through the water too quickly.

What is asthma?

Asthma is a condition in which breathing becomes very difficult. It can be triggered by breathing in particles that cause irritation, or in some cases by stress or even a change in weather conditions. During an asthma attack, the smaller air passages in the lungs become narrower and the person finds it harder to breathe. Asthma can be relieved using an inhaler containing a special spray.

What is bronchitis?

Bronchitis is an inflammation of the two large air passages—the bronchi. It happens when the bronchi become infected by harmful germs. Bronchitis can be treated with antibiotics.

What does a stethoscope do?

When a doctor uses a stethoscope she is listening to the sounds the air makes as you breathe in and out. The air should make a soft, rustling sound. Whistling or creaking noises could be a sign of infection in the lungs.

What is an iron lung?

An iron lung is a metal tank with an attached pump that changes air pressure within the tank. It is used to help patients whose chest muscles are paralyzed. This means that they cannot breathe on their own behalf. The iron lung inflates and deflates the patients' lungs for them.

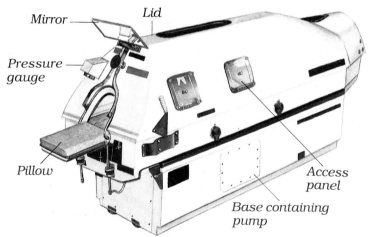

Mirror

Lid

Pressure gauge

Pillow

Access panel

Base containing pump

An iron lung works by changing the air pressure inside the tank, causing air to be drawn into the lungs.

What does a heart-lung machine do?

A heart-lung machine temporarily takes the place of these organs during a heart-lung transplant operation. During the operation, the heart-lung machine receives deoxygenated blood from the patient's major veins, adds oxygen to it, and returns the blood into the patient's main artery.

How does smoking affect breathing?

Tobacco smoke contains thick brown tar and other chemicals that stick to the insides of the air sacs and air passages. This irritates them, making breathing difficulties more likely.

What causes a smoker's cough?

Cigarette smoke paralyzes the action of the cilia in the air passages. Mucus builds up in the lungs rather than being pushed up to the throat and swallowed. The smoker may develop a hacking cough to try to move it.

Why does smoking affect fitness?

Carbon monoxide is a poisonous gas found in cigarette smoke. It limits the blood's ability to pick up oxygen. Tar and other substances in cigarette smoke build up in the air sacs and keep them from taking in oxygen as effectively. Both these things lower the amount of oxygen that can be delivered by the blood to working muscles. As a result, exercising muscles will not work as effectively.

What other effects does smoking have?

Nicotine, a highly poisonous substance found in tobacco smoke, enters the blood through the lungs. It raises blood pressure and is highly addictive. Smoking increases the chances of heart disease and cancer of the lungs, throat, and mouth, as well as other illnesses. Every year, many people die of smoking-related diseases.

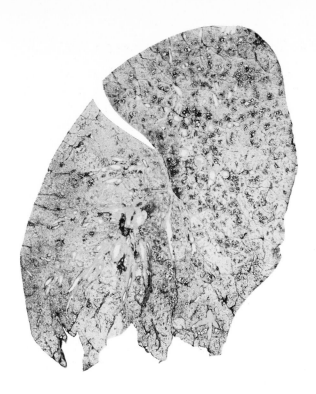

This cross-section through the blackened lung of a smoker shows deposits of soot and tar caused by cigarettes. A healthy lung is pink.

What can a chest X ray show?

Doctors use chest X rays to look for signs of disease in the lungs. The infections that cause bronchitis, pneumonia, or tuberculosis, or more serious conditions such as lung cancer, can show up on the X ray picture as a dark patch known as a shadow on the lung.

What is your Adam's apple?

Your Adam's apple is the lump in the front of your throat. It is formed by the voice box, or larynx, which sits at the top of the windpipe. Inside the larynx are two bands of cartilage called vocal cords.

What causes snoring?

The most common form of snoring is caused by soft tissues in the throat collapsing when someone falls into a deep sleep. These soft tissues partly block the passage of air into and out of the lungs, and vibrations are set up, producing the snoring sound.

Why do we yawn?

A yawn seems to be the body's way of getting more oxygen to the brain to make us feel more lively. When we yawn we take in air slowly and deeply and then breathe it out. We seem to yawn most when we are tired, bored, or sitting in a stuffy room.

What happens when I cough?

Just before you cough, you tightly close your vocal cords and tense your chest muscles. Then, when you release your vocal cords, the air comes shooting out of your lungs. Coughing is important because it removes irritating particles from your throat and air passages.

What is a hiccup?

A hiccup occurs when your diaphragm involuntarily tightens so suddenly that air rushes into your lungs and your vocal cords snap shut. You can get hiccups if you get excited or if you eat too quickly. You may be able to stop the hiccups by holding your breath for a little while.

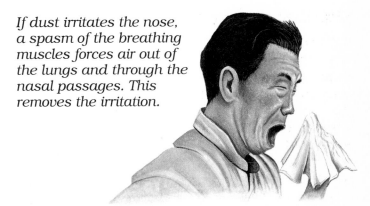

If dust irritates the nose, a spasm of the breathing muscles forces air out of the lungs and through the nasal passages. This removes the irritation.

Why do we sneeze?

Sneezing is a way of getting rid of something that is irritating the sensitive parts of the nose. Air is forced out of the lungs through the nose. Sneezing helps stop dust or pollen from reaching our lungs.

How fast is a sneeze?

When we sneeze, the air shoots out of our nose at about 100 miles an hour.

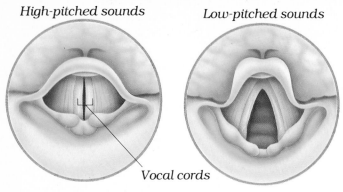

View of throat from above

High-pitched sounds   Low-pitched sounds

Vocal cords

The pitch of a note depends on the distance between the vocal cords.

How does my voice work?

When you speak or sing, air from your lungs passes out across your vocal cords and makes them vibrate. If you almost close the space between your vocal cords, you get a high-pitched sound. If you open the space, you get a lower-pitched sound. The speed of your outbreath determines how loud the note is. A fast outbreath produces a loud note. The sounds are shaped into words by your lips and tongue.

Why is my voice sometimes hoarse?

A hoarse voice can be caused by too much shouting or singing, which strains the vocal cords. Laryngitis, a condition where the larynx becomes inflamed, also causes a raspy voice, as well as a sore throat and a dry cough. If a hoarse voice lasts more than a few days, see a doctor.

What happens when we laugh?

A laugh is a long outbreath of air punctuated by a series of "ha" sounds. It is our way of expressing happiness and amusement.

What is hyperventilation?

Hyperventilation is deep or rapid breathing usually brought on by anxiety. It flushes carbon dioxide out of the body and can produce dizziness, faintness, and even muscle twitching and numbness. One way to stop it is for the person to try to relax and gradually breathe more slowly and gently.

What is anaerobic exercise?

Anaerobic exercise is exercise that uses up a lot of energy in a very short time. Your muscles use up oxygen faster than it is replaced, and so for a while the muscles release energy without using oxygen. Anaerobic exercise increases muscular strength, but is not very good for strengthening the heart and lungs. Sprinting and weight lifting are types of anaerobic exercise.

After finishing a race, a sprinter must start to "pay back" the oxygen debt by deep breathing in order to process the buildup of lactic acid.

Who pays the oxygen debt?

When you pant after a sprint, you are paying the oxygen debt. Anaerobic exercise causes a build-up of lactic acid, a waste product. Once the exercise is over, the liver processes the lactic acid, using oxygen to break it down. The oxygen debt is the amount of oxygen you must take in to process the lactic acid that has built up.

What is aerobic exercise?

Aerobic exercise is any kind of exercise that improves your ability to take in oxygen and deliver it around the body. It helps to strengthen the heart and lungs. Any fairly vigorous exercise that you do steadily for 20 minutes or more will do this—jogging, swimming, and exercise classes are all good examples.

Heart and Circulation

The main vessels in the circulation system, with arteries shown in red, and veins in blue. The heart is the pump that powers the circulation.

What is your circulation?

Your circulation is the system that carries blood around your body. It consists of a pump called the heart, and a branching system of tubes, called blood vessels.

Are all blood vessels the same?

No. There are three main types of blood vessels. Arteries carry blood away from the heart. Veins carry blood back to the heart. Capillaries are the tiny blood vessels that connect the arteries with the veins.

Is the blood in the arteries different from that in the veins?

In most cases, yes. The blood in nearly all of our arteries has come from the lungs and is rich in oxygen, low in carbon dioxide, and bright red in color. Blood in most veins carries little oxygen, a lot of carbon dioxide, and is a dark purplish color.

What happens in the capillaries?

The substances in blood are loaded and unloaded here. Oxygen passes from red blood cells through the capillary walls and on into the surrounding tissues. At the same time, carbon dioxide and other wastes pass from the surrounding tissues into the blood. The exception is in the lungs; there, capillaries pick up oxygen and unload carbon dioxide.

How thick is a capillary?

Ten capillaries bunched together would be much thinner than a human hair. A single capillary is about 0.0004 inch across and has a very thin wall made up of a single layer of cells. The thin wall means that chemicals can pass easily in and out of the capillary. This is very important because the blood needs to pick up chemicals in some parts of the body and get rid of chemicals in other parts.

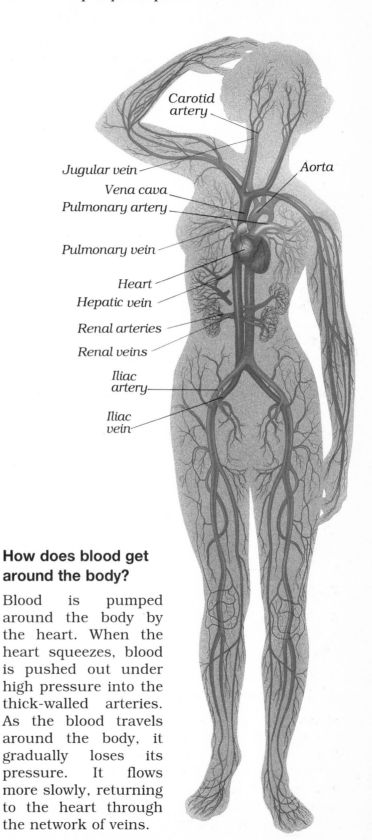

Carotid artery

Jugular vein

Aorta

Vena cava

Pulmonary artery

Pulmonary vein

Heart

Hepatic vein

Renal arteries

Renal veins

Iliac artery

Iliac vein

How does blood get around the body?

Blood is pumped around the body by the heart. When the heart squeezes, blood is pushed out under high pressure into the thick-walled arteries. As the blood travels around the body, it gradually loses its pressure. It flows more slowly, returning to the heart through the network of veins.

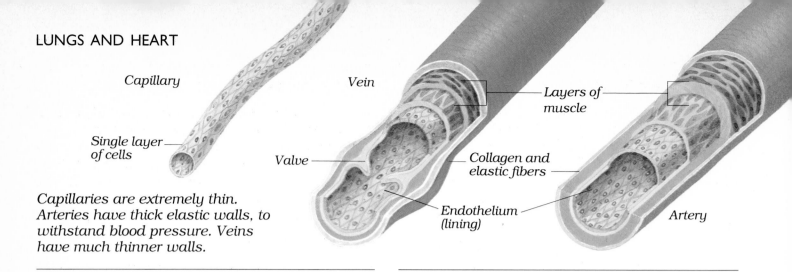

Capillary

Vein

Layers of muscle

Single layer of cells

Valve

Collagen and elastic fibers

Endothelium (lining)

Artery

Capillaries are extremely thin. Arteries have thick elastic walls, to withstand blood pressure. Veins have much thinner walls.

What is the difference between an artery and a vein?

Arteries carry blood away from the heart at high pressure. They have thick muscular walls to withstand this pressure. Veins carry blood back to the heart at low pressure and so have thinner walls. They also contain one-way valves to help direct the flow of blood back to the heart.

What route does blood take around the body?

Starting from the right side of the heart, blood travels to the lungs. There it is filled with oxygen and returned to the left side of the heart. The oxygenated blood is pumped through arteries to the body's organs and muscles, where the oxygen is unloaded. Veins then carry the deoxygenated blood back to the right side of the heart.

How fast does blood flow?

Blood leaves the heart at about the rate of 3 feet per second, but it slows down as it enters the smaller arteries. It takes about one minute for a drop of blood to travel from the heart down to your toes and back again.

How does the heart work?

Each side of the heart has two chambers. The top chambers, called atria (the singular is atrium), receive blood from large veins. When the atria squeeze, they pump blood into the bottom chambers, or ventricles. The ventricles then squeeze, pumping blood along large arteries. One-way valves make sure that blood flows through the heart in only one direction.

Is the heart one pump or two?

The heart is really two separate pumps, one on the right, and one on the left. The pump on the left pumps blood around the entire body; the pump on the right pumps blood to the lungs.

The heart is a muscular organ that must work without stopping throughout your life.

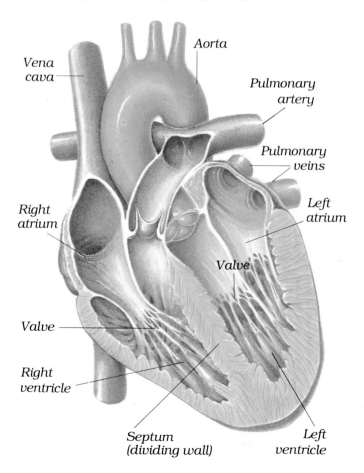

Aorta

Vena cava

Pulmonary artery

Pulmonary veins

Right atrium

Left atrium

Valve

Valve

Right ventricle

Septum (dividing wall)

Left ventricle

Why does the heart have chambers?

The heart has four chambers (two on each side) so that blood can enter the heart at the same time as blood is being pumped out. The atrium is a temporary blood store that fills up with blood in preparation for delivery to the ventricle.

How big is the heart?

In an adult the heart is about the size of a fist and weighs about 10 ounces. Your heart is found in the middle of your chest, set very slightly to the left.

Is my heart heart-shaped?

Not exactly. The shape of a "love heart" is only roughly similar to a real heart. Inside the body the heart is tilted, and the left side is slightly bigger than the right. With all the blood vessels going in and out of the top of the heart, the basic "heart" shape tends to be obscured.

What is the heart made of?

The heart is made mostly of special muscle called cardiac muscle. This contracts automatically to pump blood around the body. It also contains valves made of strong fibrous tissue, as well as some nervous tissue that controls the speed as well as the strength of the heart's pumping.

What are my "heartstrings"?

Your heartstrings are the tendons that are attached to the heart valves lying between the atria and ventricles. The valves prevent the blood from flowing backward into the atria from the ventricles. The tendons stop the valves from turning inside out.

What is a heartbeat?

A heartbeat is the sound the heart makes when the heart valves open and close. One heartbeat equals one squeeze of the atria and ventricles. A doctor places a stethoscope on the front of your chest to hear these sounds clearly and check the health of your heart.

What is the pacemaker?

The pacemaker is a specialized patch of cells on the heart. These cells control heart rate. The pacemaker receives messages from nerves and hormones, and these may change heart rate. Artificial pacemakers work electronically to carry out the same task.

How can I measure my heart rate?

The easiest way to measure your heart rate is by measuring your pulse. The pulse is a regular throb or beat which can be felt beneath the skin at certain points. Your heart rate equals the number of pulses that can be counted in one minute.

What causes the pulse?

When our heart beats and blood is pumped out into our arteries, the arteries stretch and bulge. This stretching with each heartbeat is the pulse. It can be felt in places where arteries are close to the surface of the skin.

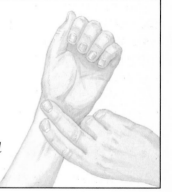

Taking your pulse

Place the fingers of one hand just below the wrist on the other—you will feel a throb beneath your skin. To find your heart rate, count the number of times you feel this in a minute.

Does my heart rate go up after a meal?

Yes. Your heart rate goes up after you have eaten because extra blood is pumped to the digestive tract, to pick up food that you have just digested.

What are your coronary arteries?

The coronary arteries are blood vessels that form a network over the surface of the heart. Even though your heart is full of blood, your heart muscles need their own blood supply to provide the food and oxygen they need. The blood is provided by the coronary arteries.

What is blood made of?

Blood consists of a liquid called plasma, which contains red and white blood cells, and cell fragments called platelets. Dissolved in the plasma are thousands of different substances.

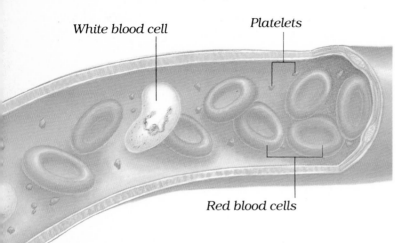

White blood cell   Platelets

Red blood cells

In blood, the cells that transport oxygen and fight disease are suspended in a liquid called plasma.

What is blood for?

Blood has four main jobs: transport, protection, communication, and temperature regulation. Blood carries useful materials around the body and takes away waste products. Blood protects the body from germs by sealing cuts with thickened, or clotted, blood and by using white blood cells to kill germs. Blood helps with communication by delivering chemical messengers called hormones to parts of the body. Finally, body temperature can be controlled by directing blood to or away from the skin.

Why is blood red?

Blood is red because of the presence of a colored substance called hemoglobin in the red blood cells. Hemoglobin contains iron, and it is iron that gives blood its red color.

Does blood change color?

Yes. When blood is low in oxygen, the hemoglobin is dark purplish red in color. When blood is full of oxygen, the hemoglobin becomes bright red.

What do red blood cells do?

The main function of red blood cells is to deliver oxygen around the body. The hemoglobin in red blood cells combines with oxygen, which is picked up in the lungs and then delivered to all body tissues. Hemoglobin is a very efficient oxygen carrier. It allows blood to carry 60 times more oxygen than could be dissolved in the blood plasma.

What shape is a red blood cell?

A red blood cell is the shape of a ring doughnut with the hole filled in, but on a microscopic scale (a red blood cell measures 3 thousandths of an inch across). The special shape of a red blood cell gives it a large surface area for taking in oxygen. The shape also makes the cells flexible so that they can squeeze through narrow spaces, such as the insides of capillaries.

How are red blood cells unique?

Red blood cells are the only cells in the body that do not have a nucleus. This means that the whole of the inside of the cell can be packed full of hemoglobin. However, it also means that they are very short-lived.

What do white blood cells do?

White blood cells help protect the body from disease. About two-thirds of white blood cells are called phagocytes. They help defend the body by eating up invading germs. The other white cells are called lymphocytes. They produce chemicals called antibodies, which also destroy harmful germs. White blood cells are much larger than red blood cells, but there are fewer of them.

Phagocytes are able to surround, and eventually destroy, bacteria.

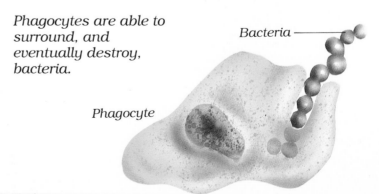

Bacteria

Phagocyte

What are platelets?

Platelets are cell fragments. They are the smallest particles in blood and are essential for blood clotting.

What does plasma carry?

Plasma is about 90 percent water, in which thousands of substances are dissolved. These include foods for energy, waste products, antibodies, and the body's chemical messengers, called hormones.

Where does blood come from?

Blood is constantly being made and replaced. The water in blood plasma originally comes from food and drink. Red cells, platelets, and some kinds of white blood cells are made by bone marrow inside some of the long bones. Other types of white blood cells are made in special clumps of tissue, called lymph nodes, which are found throughout the body.

How much blood is in the body?

A baby has about 1 quart of blood, a child about 3 quarts, and an adult about 5 quarts.

What part of the body gets the most blood?

Pound for pound, the kidneys get more blood than other organs. The kidneys have a vital role in filtering and cleaning the blood.

Do the kidneys get more blood all the time?

No. During hard exercise, the body supplies the muscles with up to five times more blood than when the body is at rest. Blood is diverted from other organs to feed the muscles. Only the blood supply to the brain is constant.

This chart shows how blood is diverted from other organs to feed the muscles during exercise.

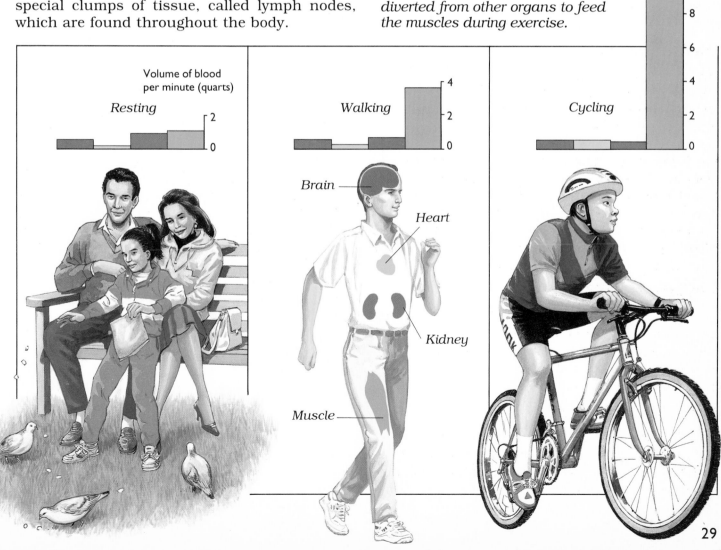

Volume of blood per minute (quarts)

Resting

Walking

Cycling

Brain

Heart

Kidney

Muscle

Where is the vena cava?

The vena cava is found just above the right side of the heart. It is in fact two veins, the inferior vena cava and the superior vena cava. These are the largest veins in the body.

How wide is the aorta?

The aorta is about 1 inch across, making it the largest artery in the body. When you are at rest the aorta carries blood at the rate of about 5 quarts a minute. As it leaves the heart the aorta points upward. It then loops back down in a bend called the aortic arch.

What is special about the pulmonary artery?

The pulmonary artery is the only artery that carries deoxygenated blood (blood that is low in oxygen). This is because it is the blood vessel that carries blood to the lungs to pick up oxygen. Likewise, the pulmonary vein is the only vein that carries oxygenated blood (blood that is rich in oxygen), because it carries blood away from the lungs after it has picked up oxygen.

How long are all my blood vessels?

Adding together every capillary, vein, and artery, the length of all the blood vessels in your body is about 60,000 miles—nearly two and a half times the distance around the world.

Why do cuts stop bleeding?

Cuts stop bleeding because blood quickly forms a clot that plugs the wound and seals off the damaged blood vessels.

What causes blood to clot?

At the site of an injury, the platelets in the bloodstream stick together and stick to the edges of the cut, making a thin seal. At the same time the platelets and damaged cells at the site of the injury release substances that react with clotting factors in the blood. This leads to the formation of fibers. Blood cells get caught up in the tangle of platelets and fibers and form a clot that plugs the leak.

How does blood help eliminate germs?

When we cut or graze our skin, blood vessels break. Blood leaks out and helps wash harmful germs from the site of the injury. Platelets help form a clot, which later becomes a scab and seals up the injury. At the same time, the phagocytes move in and eat up any germs that may have entered the body, while the lymphocytes knock out the germs by producing the disease-fighting chemicals called antibodies.

What is a blood group?

A blood group is the name given to a particular type of blood. Blood groups differ from person to person. The two main systems for grouping blood are the ABO and the Rhesus systems.

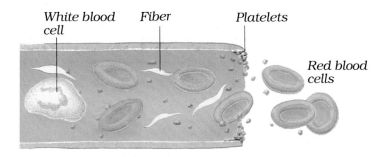

Blood leaks from the broken vessel at a cut. Germs may enter the body at the wound.

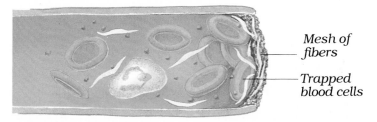

The platelets seal the cut and at the same time trigger the blood to produce fibers.

The fibers trap red blood cells, which begin to clot together to plug the site of the injury.

How many different blood groups are there?

There are four blood groups in the most common system of blood grouping—the ABO system. The four groups are O, A, B, and AB. These letters refer to types of chemicals found on the surface of red blood cells.

What is a blood transfusion?

A blood transfusion is the transfer of blood from a healthy person into the body of someone who lacks enough blood, either because of disease or injury. The donor's blood must be matched to the patient's blood group.

What is the danger of mixing blood groups?

When blood from two different groups is mixed, mismatching may occur, causing the blood to clot. If someone is given a transfusion of mismatched blood, the result could be fatal. Therefore, blood is carefully checked before being used in a transfusion.

What is a blood donor?

A blood donor is someone who gives their own blood voluntarily so that hospitals can have a supply stored, ready for operations and emergencies. A donor can give about a pint of blood without any ill effect. The blood is taken from a vein in the arm.

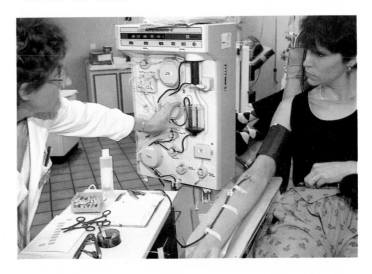

Blood from donors is stored and then used when needed in transfusions.

Blood group	Reacts against	Can give blood to	Can receive blood from
A	B	A AB	A O
B	A	B AB	O B
AB	NONE	AB	A B AB O
O	A B	A B AB O	O

Blood group O can be given to people of all blood groups without the risk of clotting. A patient with blood group AB can receive blood from any group.

What is blood serum?

Blood serum is blood plasma from which the clotting factors have been removed. It is the clear liquid that oozes from the skin after you cut yourself. Blood plasma can be used in certain types of blood transfusions.

What is the Rhesus factor?

Blood can also be grouped according to the Rhesus (Rh) factor. People are either Rh-positive or Rh-negative—most people (about 85 percent) are Rh-positive. Mixing the two types can be dangerous. For example, if an Rh-negative woman is pregnant for the second time with a child who is Rh-positive, then without treatment the child may suffer from brain damage.

What is blood pressure?

Blood pressure is the pushing force given to blood by the heart. A doctor usually measures blood pressure with a special arm cuff attached to a gauge. Two readings are taken. The first reading gives blood pressure during heartbeats; the second gives pressure between heartbeats. These readings tell a doctor about the health of your heart and circulation.

What is anemia?

Anemia is a condition that occurs when there is not enough iron in the body to make healthy red blood cells. As a result, not enough oxygen is delivered around the body. A person who is anemic may look pale, feel tired, and have no energy. Extra iron in tablets, or in the right kind of food, usually solves the problem. Meat, eggs, grains, and spinach are good sources of iron.

What is hemophilia?

Hemophilia is a condition in which the blood fails to clot properly. For people with this condition, it can be difficult to stop a cut from bleeding. Before transfusions were widely available hemophiliacs could not lead normal, active lives. Nowadays they can have injections of a specialized substance so that their blood will be able to clot if they cut themselves.

Hemophilia is a disease handed down through families. In Great Britain, Queen Victoria's son Leopold, and several grandchildren, were sufferers.

What is leukemia?

Leukemia is a cancer of the bone marrow that results in too many white blood cells being produced. Some forms of leukemia can be treated with special chemicals or with radiation followed by bone marrow transplants.

What is blood poisoning?

Blood poisoning is an infection that has spread in the blood, perhaps caused by an infected cut. It can be treated with antibiotics.

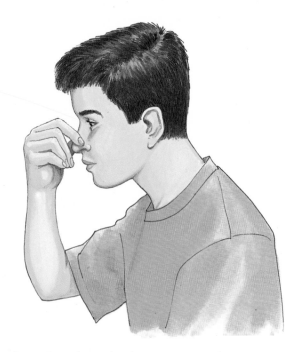

Pinching hard on the lower half of your nose should help stop a nosebleed.

What causes nosebleeds?

There are many causes of nosebleeds, as the blood vessels in the nose are particularly delicate. Blowing your nose too hard or even a change in the weather can cause a nosebleed.

How can I stop a nosebleed?

If you have a nosebleed, sit down and bend forward. Pinch hard on the lower half of your nose for 10 minutes without letting go. This helps the blood clot. If the bleeding does not stop, or if you think your nose might be broken, see a doctor.

What is a stroke?

A stroke is a sudden interruption of the blood supply to the brain. It occurs when blood vessels in the brain are blocked or have burst. When food and oxygen cannot reach part of the brain, the brain cells in that region die.

What is a hemorrhage?

When a blood vessel is damaged and blood flows out of it freely, the blood is lost from the circulation. It can no longer carry oxygen or food around the body to the cells. This is a hemorrhage. It could occur at a cut, a bruise, or a burst blood vessel.

What is a "hole in the heart"?

All babies are born with a "hole in the heart," but in most cases it closes up with the first few breaths. It is a break in the middle wall that separates the two sides of the heart. If the hole does not close up, as sometimes happens, used blood mixes with blood rich in oxygen. This stops the heart from pumping properly. Surgeons can operate to close up the hole.

If a hole in the wall that separates the two ventricles does not close up, blood from the left and right sides mixes, putting a strain on the lungs.

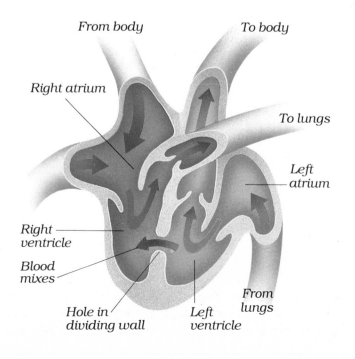

From body

To body

Right atrium

To lungs

Left atrium

Right ventricle

Blood mixes

Hole in dividing wall

Left ventricle

From lungs

What causes a heart attack?

A heart attack occurs when the heart can no longer cope with the demands made upon it and cannot keep up its normal rhythm. Heart attacks are usually caused by a blood clot blocking a coronary artery. Some heart muscle cells become starved of food and oxygen, and die. Although a heart attack can kill, often people do recover from them.

What is "hardening of the arteries"?

It is when fats and other substances build up on the inside of the arteries. The artery walls become rigid and cannot expand to allow enough blood to pass through them. This makes heart attacks and other heart conditions more likely to occur.

Why can cholesterol cause heart disease?

Cholesterol is a fatty substance found in some foods. Your body also makes it. Inside the body cholesterol can collect on the inner surface of blood vessels. This can lead to the formation of blood clots, which break off and block other vessels. If this occurs in one of the coronary arteries, a heart attack can result.

What makes your heart flutter?

A pounding or racing of the heart is called a heart flutter. Your heart can flutter when you are worried or excited. It is perfectly natural. Some types of heart condition cause a person to have heart flutters quite often.

What is angina?

Angina is a pain in the chest usually caused by insufficient oxygen reaching the heart muscle. It may occur in middle-aged or older people and is often a sign of hardening of the coronary arteries (the blood vessels around the heart).

How successful are heart transplant operations?

About 80 percent of patients who receive a new heart survive a year or more after the operation.

FOOD and WASTE

Why do we need food?

Food contains different kinds of substances that our bodies need as raw materials for energy, growth, and repair.

What is digestion?

Digestion is the process that breaks down food into units that can be taken into and used by your body. The food is first chewed into smaller pieces. Then it is broken down chemically in the stomach and intestines by special proteins called digestive enzymes.

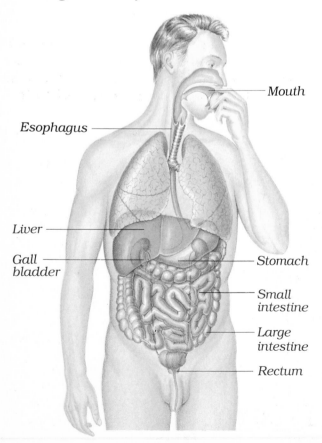

Mouth

Esophagus

Liver

Gall bladder

Stomach

Small intestine

Large intestine

Rectum

What is the alimentary canal?

The alimentary canal, or digestive tract, is a long tube inside your body that runs from your mouth to your anus. It is in the alimentary canal that digestion takes place.

What would happen if we did not eat?

If you stopped taking food into your body, you would soon start to feel listless. If you went without food for long enough, you would start to lose weight. Your body would fail to work normally and you would eventually die.

What is in our food?

There are seven major types of substances in our food. Fats, proteins, and carbohydrates are the three main types. Vitamins and minerals are found in small amounts. Most of our food also contains water, and some contains fiber, which we cannot digest.

Why do we need protein?

Protein is essential to all living things. It is a body-building substance found in many foods, including cheese, eggs, fish, meat, and soy products. All proteins are made of chemical units called amino acids. After the protein is digested, amino acids are taken up into the blood and carried to all cells to be made into new proteins. This helps the body grow and repair itself.

In the digestive system food is broken down into nutrient materials that the body can use for energy and growth.

Bread

Grains

Eggs

Nuts

Meat

Fish

Butter

Cheese

Fruit

Vegetables

Which foods give us energy?

Foods that contain carbohydrates are a good source of energy. Sugars and a substance called starch, found in bread and potatoes, are carbohydrates. Fats give us energy too. Butter, margarine, and oils are very rich in fats. They should be eaten in small amounts.

What is fiber?

Fiber, or roughage, is the part of food that you cannot digest. It is mostly made up of the walls of plant cells. Fiber adds bulk to the food in our digestive tract and helps the intestine squeeze it through our system more easily.

Which foods contain the most fiber?

Vegetables and fruits are good sources of fiber, as are any whole-grain products (seeds such as wheat, oats, and brown rice).

Why do we need vitamins and minerals?

Although we need only tiny amounts of vitamins and minerals, they are essential for many functions in the body. Lack of the mineral iron, for example, leads to a shortage of red blood cells. This causes anemia.

Which vitamin helps our bones grow?

Vitamin D helps our bones develop. Lack of vitamin D leads to brittle bones and, in children, rickets, a condition in which the legs become bowed. Vitamin D is found in fish and cheese, and is made by the skin in sunlight.

Meat, fish, nuts, eggs, and cheese supply us with protein. Fats, bread, and grains give us carbohydrates. Fruits and vegetables provide vitamins, minerals, and fiber.

What is scurvy?

Scurvy is a rare disease caused by a lack of vitamin C. People with scurvy have gums that bleed easily and bruises and skin wounds that do not heal properly. Vitamin C is found in most fresh fruits, salads, and vegetables.

What is a balanced diet?

A balanced diet is one that supplies the different types of foods needed in the right amounts—not too much and not too little of any. It provides the raw materials and energy required for a healthy, active life.

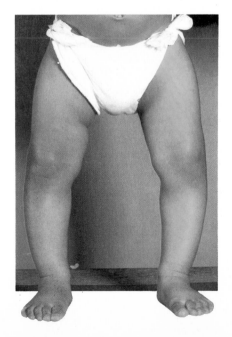

This child is suffering from rickets, a disease caused by a lack of vitamin D. Without vitamin D there is not enough calcium in the diet to make bones rigid. The bones in the leg are bent out of shape under the weight of the child's body.

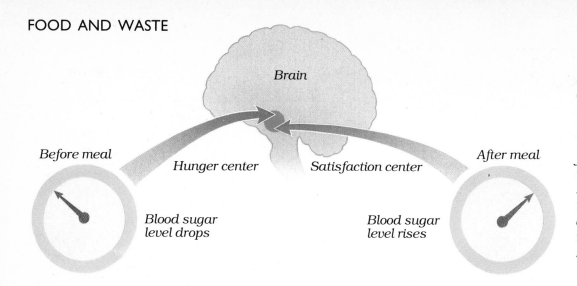

Brain

Before meal

Hunger center   Satisfaction center

After meal

Blood sugar level drops

Blood sugar level rises

When the level of sugar in our blood drops, receptors in the brain send a signal to the hunger center. When the stomach is full, stretch receptors in the stomach walls send this information to the satisfaction center in the brain, so that we know when to stop eating.

How much food do I need in a day?

The amount of food you need each day depends on your age, size, and sex, as well as your general level of activity. A tall teenage boy who plays a lot of sports needs a lot more food each day than a small elderly woman.

What is a calorie?

A calorie, or kilocalorie (kcal), is a unit of energy. The energy value of food is measured in calories. A peanut, for example, contains about 5 calories. A man needs about 3,000 calories a day, a woman about 2,500.

Why do people become overweight?

The simple answer is because they take in more energy in their food than they burn up. This extra energy is converted to fat and stored in the body, often just under the skin.

Why can some people eat a lot without getting fat?

Some people seem able to burn up lots of food inside their bodies. This means they do not have any food left over to store as fat. Such people seem to have lots of brown fat cells—special cells that burn up fat.

How much food do we eat in a lifetime?

The average person living in a wealthy industrialized Western country eats about 30 tons of food in a lifetime.

Why do we get hungry?

Our eating is controlled by an area deep in the brain. When this "hunger center" receives signals from parts of the body saying that we need to eat, we get hungry. Painful sensations, such as stomach cramps, prompt us to eat.

Why do we feel full?

When our stomach is full of food or drink the stomach walls become stretched. This sends signals to an area of our brain that tells us to stop eating.

Why do we eat three meals a day?

This is partly out of habit. However, having meals spread throughout the day at regular intervals allows our digestive system to work efficiently on the food that we eat. Eating smaller amounts of food more often is much better than trying to eat a large amount at one sitting.

What causes thirst?

We feel thirsty when the normal amount of water in the blood starts to drop, and the blood gets somewhat thicker. Part of our brain senses this and sends signals to the body that tell us we need more fluid.

How much water do we need every day?

An adult needs about 1.5 to 2 quarts of water a day. Much of this will come from food. For example, bread is about 40 percent water.

Teeth

Why do we need teeth?

Without teeth, people could not eat food that needed to be chewed into smaller pieces. They could only eat soft foods or liquids.

Why are teeth different shapes?

Teeth are different shapes because they have different jobs to do. The incisor teeth at the front of your mouth are shaped like chisels. They are used for biting and gnawing. The canines, just behind the incisors, are pointed teeth used for tearing food. The premolars and molars at the back are shaped for grinding.

How do our teeth work as a team?

Our teeth work as a team to break down food. You use your incisors and canines to take a bite of food. You then use your premolars and molars to grind it up.

Are teeth alive?

The enamel coat of a tooth is not alive, but the layers underneath it are. The layers toward the center of the tooth are more sensitive.

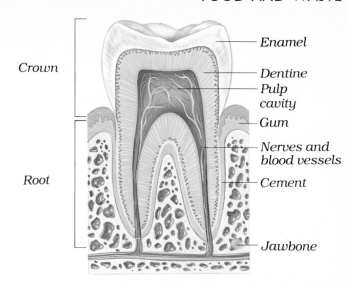

Tough enamel, made of minerals and keratin, protects the dentine and soft pulp in our teeth.

What are teeth made of?

Each tooth consists of a visible part, called the crown, and a root, which attaches it to a socket in the jawbone. The outer, off-white part of the tooth is made of enamel, the hardest substance in the body. Underneath the enamel is dentine, which is similar to bone, but harder. At the center of the tooth is a soft core containing blood vessels and nerve endings.

How do teeth grow?

Teeth grow from small patches of tissue covering the bone of the upper and lower jaws. Teeth start growing before we are born, but they only begin to come through the gum about six months after birth.

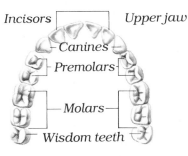

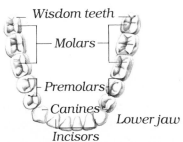

Left: An adult with a full set of teeth has 16 in each jaw. The third molars, or wisdom teeth, do not always come through.

Right: Flat incisors are used to cut food, canines are used for tearing, and the ridged premolars and molars crush and grind food into small pieces.

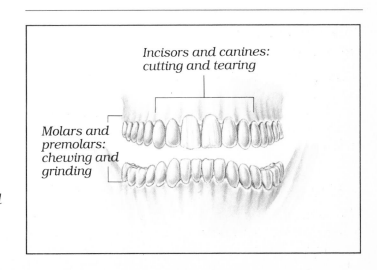

Why do we chew food?

Chewing is the first stage of digestion. We chew our food to break it down so we can swallow it. Chewing also mixes the food with saliva to moisten it, which makes it easier to swallow.

What are baby teeth?

Baby teeth are our first set of teeth. A child's baby teeth usually come through by the age of two. Children up to the age of about six have 20 teeth, 10 in each jaw. After the age of six the baby teeth begin to fall out and are replaced by permanent teeth.

What are wisdom teeth?

Wisdom teeth are the last permanent teeth to come through. Some people never grow them at all. Wisdom teeth are the four molars that come through right at the back of the mouth and often do not appear until early adulthood. By that time we are supposed to have gained some wisdom!

What is saliva?

Saliva is the colorless fluid produced in our mouth. It comes from groups of cells called glands found under the tongue and in the cheeks. Saliva is mostly water, with some mucus. It also contains an enzyme that starts off the digestive process by breaking down starch, a carbohydrate.

Why does my mouth water?

The taste, smell, and sometimes even the thought of food causes the salivary glands to send saliva along little ducts into the mouth. Sometimes this happens with such force that jets of saliva squirt out into your mouth, so that your mouth "waters."

What happens when I swallow?

Swallowing is a complicated process. When you swallow, your tongue squeezes against the roof of your mouth and pushes the food or drink up and back. At the same time, the soft part at the top of your mouth moves up, closing off the nasal passages so that nothing goes up your nose. Finally, your epiglottis flaps down and your larynx (voice box) moves forward and upward. This closes off the windpipe and opens up the gullet, or esophagus. The food or drink is squeezed into your throat and travels down the esophagus to reach the stomach.

Can I swallow upside-down?

Yes, you can, but it is not a good idea to try it since you might choke. It is possible to swallow upside-down because food does not just fall down the esophagus into the stomach. It is pushed there by circular bands of muscle in the walls of the esophagus. These contract behind the food, squeezing it along. This action is called peristalsis. Food moves along the tubes of the entire digestive system by peristalsis.

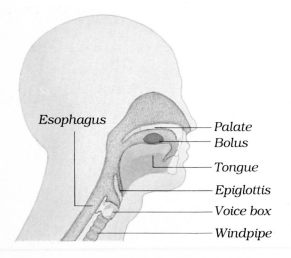

Esophagus — Palate / Bolus / Tongue / Epiglottis / Voice box / Windpipe

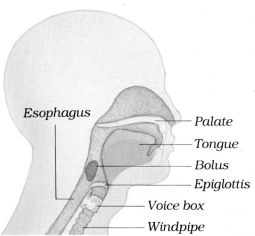

Esophagus — Palate / Tongue / Bolus / Epiglottis / Voice box / Windpipe

The tongue shapes food into a ball, or bolus, and pushes it to the back of the mouth so it can be swallowed. The epiglottis flaps down and closes off the windpipe, making sure that food does not go down the wrong way.

Digesting Food

Where does digestion begin?

Digestion begins in the mouth. From here, food travels to the stomach, then through a long tube called the small intestine. This is where most digestion takes place. Finally, the large intestine, or colon, takes up water from the food.

What does the stomach look like?

The stomach looks like the bag of a bagpipe. It has muscular walls and is closed by valves.

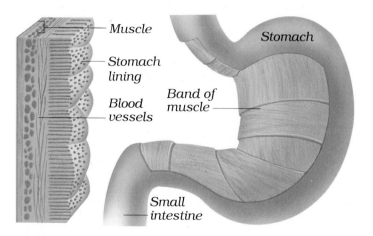

A stomach can hold about 1.5 quarts of food. Contractions of its muscular walls churn up the food, mixing it with digestive juices.

What happens in the stomach?

In the stomach, food is churned up and mixed with stomach juices containing digestive enzymes and acid. These continue to break down the food chemically, turning it into a pulpy liquid. The acid also kills most of the germs in food. The liquid is then delivered gradually to the small intestine.

Why doesn't the stomach digest itself?

The walls of the stomach are protected from the enzymes and strong acid in the stomach juices by a thick layer of mucus. This keeps the stomach from digesting itself.

Why does my tummy sometimes rumble?

The stomach and intestines are very active. The stomach churns food and the intestines squeeze it along. All this activity means that your stomach makes noises most of the time. When you are hungry your stomach contains a little liquid and a lot of gas. Because there is a lot of gas in your stomach, its rumblings are louder.

What happens to food in the small intestine?

Most of the digestion process takes place in the small intestine. This is also where most food is taken up, or absorbed, into the blood. The small intestine has digestive juices emptied into it that break down the proteins, carbohydrates, and fats in the food into smaller units that can be absorbed into the blood.

How is food absorbed into the blood?

Millions of tiny, finger-like bumps called villi (singular, villus) line the small intestine. Villi contain tiny blood vessels that absorb food.

How small is the small intestine?

Not as small as it sounds! The first part of the small intestine, the duodenum, is about 12 inches long and 1 inch wide. The rest of the small intestine is about 20 feet long.

Digestive enzymes break down fats, proteins, and carbohydrates into small units that are absorbed into the blood through villi in the intestine wall.

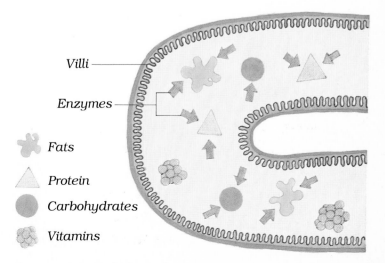

Where does absorbed food go?

The food is taken into the blood in the form of simple chemicals and carried to the liver.

What does the liver do?

The liver has many roles. One of its most important tasks is to process digested food and store it or distribute it to the body. The liver also breaks down fats, helps rid the body of poisons, makes important blood proteins, and stores vitamins and iron.

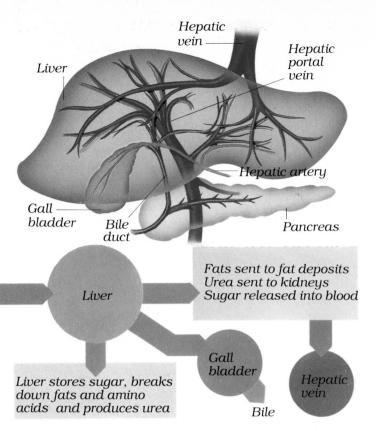

Food absorbed from the small intestine is transported to the liver, which processes digested food and cleans poisons from the blood. It also makes bile, which is stored in the gall bladder and passes to the intestine along the bile duct.

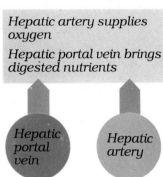

Hepatic artery supplies oxygen

Hepatic portal vein brings digested nutrients

Hepatic portal vein

Hepatic artery

Liver

Liver stores sugar, breaks down fats and amino acids and produces urea

Gall bladder

Bile

Fats sent to fat deposits
Urea sent to kidneys
Sugar released into blood

Hepatic vein

Which foods does the liver process?

The liver processes the digestion products of all the major food groups. If we have excess protein in our diet, the body cannot store the extra amino acids. So the liver breaks them down, burning up part of the acids for energy and forming a waste product called urea. The liver converts excess carbohydrates into a form of starch called glycogen and stores it for later use as a source of energy. Some fats are "burned," or respired, for energy, some are stored, and some are chemically changed and sent off in the bloodstream to all parts of the body.

How does the liver get rid of poisons?

Chemical reactions in the body may produce poisonous substances, or toxins, as by-products. Some of our food may also have toxic contents. The liver turns many of these toxins into harmless substances. These are either put to some other use, or simply sent to the kidney to be excreted. This process is called detoxification.

What is bile?

Bile is a liquid produced by the liver, partly from old red blood cells. It is stored in the gall bladder and squirted into the small intestine along the bile duct. Bile breaks up fats into small droplets, which makes them easier to digest.

What color is bile?

Bile varies in color from brown to greenish-yellow. The color is due to two chemicals, one red, called bilirubin, the other green, called biliverdin. These chemicals are formed when the liver breaks down the red pigment hemoglobin in worn-out red blood cells. The liver then excretes these substances in bile.

What is jaundice?

Jaundice is not a disease itself, but is a sign of liver disease. When someone has jaundice their skin and the whites of their eyes turn yellow. The yellow color is due to a buildup of bilirubin and biliverdin in the bloodstream. The liver normally gets rid of these as bile.

What is cirrhosis of the liver?

Cirrhosis occurs when the inside of the liver is damaged; for example, by regularly drinking large amounts of alcohol. Scar tissue forms, and the damaged liver cannot carry out its functions properly.

What is the pancreas?

The pancreas is an organ near the stomach. It produces pancreatic juice, which contains many of the digestive enzymes that are emptied into the small intestine to break down food.

Where are the islets of Langerhans?

The islets of Langerhans are found in the pancreas. They produce insulin (see page 51).

How big is the large intestine?

The large intestine is shorter but wider than the small intestine. It is about 6 feet long and 2 inches wide. It is also called the colon.

What happens in the large intestine?

Inside the large intestine, bacteria help to break down the remains of food received from the small intestine. Water and minerals released from the food are absorbed through the lining of the large intestine. Solid waste is stored in the rectum and is finally passed out through the anus.

Why do we have an appendix?

The appendix is probably a left-over organ that was of use to our very distant ancestors. It is an extension of the large intestine and is about 4 inches long. In mammals such as rabbits, which eat lots of plant material, the appendix is much bigger and contains bacteria that are used to break down tough plant-cell walls. In humans it no longer has any use.

What is appendicitis?

Appendicitis is an inflammation of the appendix. The appendix may be removed by surgery without causing the person ill effect.

How long does it take to digest a meal?

It takes about 24 hours to completely digest a typical meal. Food spends about four hours in your stomach. This is followed by up to six hours in the small intestine, six or seven hours in the colon, and six or seven hours in the rectum, before the waste is expelled as feces.

A meal spends 24 hours in the digestive system. Your breakfast stays in your stomach for about four hours, then passes to the small intestine just before noon. In the early evening, what remains of your meal enters the large intestine, then passes to the rectum late at night, where it is stored until morning.

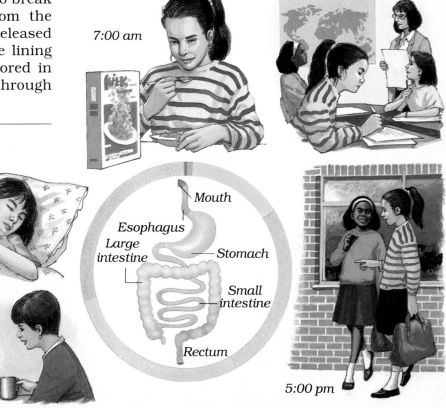

7:00 am   *11:00 am*   *12:00 am*   *8:00 pm*   *5:00 pm*

Mouth
Esophagus
Large intestine
Stomach
Small intestine
Rectum

Getting Rid of Waste

What is excretion?

Excretion is the way the body gets rid of waste substances produced by its cells.

What are the body's waste substances?

The body's main waste substances are the gas carbon dioxide (produced during respiration), urea (from breaking down excess proteins), and water and salts that the body does not need.

What are the excretory organs?

The excretory organs excrete waste. They are the lungs, the kidneys, the liver, and the skin. The lungs get rid of carbon dioxide. The kidneys and skin get rid of water and other substances, such as salts. Waste products from the liver are either taken to the kidney and excreted in urine or excreted in bile and expelled from the body through the large intestine.

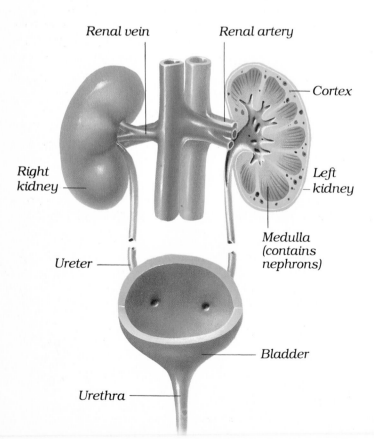

Renal vein — Renal artery — Cortex — Right kidney — Left kidney — Medulla (contains nephrons) — Ureter — Bladder — Urethra

Is the large intestine an excretory organ?

Strangely, the large intestine is not normally considered to be an excretory organ. Most of the waste in the large intestine has come not from cells in the body, but from food that cannot be digested. Waste that has not come from cells inside the body is not said to be excreted.

Where are our kidneys?

The kidneys are attached to the back wall of the abdomen, one on either side of the backbone. Each kidney is about 4 inches long and 2.5 inches wide.

What do the kidneys do?

The kidneys are a pair of very hard-working filters. They purify the blood, taking out waste substances and making sure that useful substances are kept in.

How much blood do our kidneys filter?

Our kidneys filter all the blood in our body about 300 times each day. That is the same as filtering 150 quarts of blood.

What is urine?

Urine is the fluid made in the kidneys. It contains waste substances filtered from blood. Urine empties out of each kidney along a tube called a ureter. From here it passes to the bladder, where it is stored until it leaves the body through a tube called the urethra.

What does urine contain?

Urine is a watery solution containing many wastes and other substances, such as salts. If the wastes were not expelled they would poison us. Urine is yellow because it contains substances formed by the liver when it breaks down hemoglobin from old blood cells.

Urine passes from the kidneys to the bladder along the ureters. The bladder is a muscular sac that can store about 1 pint of urine.

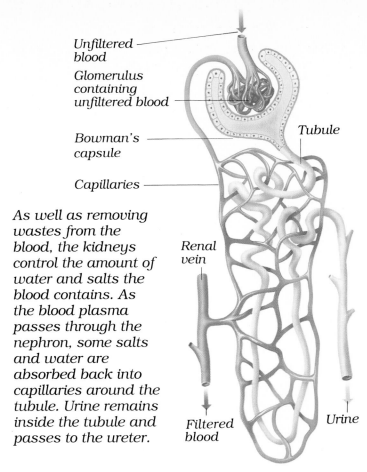

Unfiltered blood

Glomerulus containing unfiltered blood

Bowman's capsule

Capillaries

Tubule

Renal vein

Filtered blood

Urine

As well as removing wastes from the blood, the kidneys control the amount of water and salts the blood contains. As the blood plasma passes through the nephron, some salts and water are absorbed back into capillaries around the tubule. Urine remains inside the tubule and passes to the ureter.

Where would you find a glomerulus?

Each kidney has millions of tiny filtering units called nephrons. The glomerulus is a bundle of tiny blood vessels at the top of each nephron.

What is a Bowman's capsule?

A Bowman's capsule is the microscopic cup-shaped structure that is wrapped around each glomerulus in the kidney. Each Bowman's capsule leads to a long, U-shaped tube (the tubule) where the blood is filtered.

How does the kidney filter blood?

Blood arrives at the glomerulus under high pressure so that much of the blood plasma is squeezed out of the capillaries into the Bowman's capsule. As the filtered liquid passes down through the nephron, water and salts are taken back into the blood through a network of surrounding capillaries. Waste substances and some water stay inside the nephron and pass into the center of the kidney to form urine. Urine passes out of the kidney through the ureter.

What is a kidney stone?

A kidney stone is a hard mass of minerals deposited in the kidney. Kidney fluids contain many dissolved substances, such as calcium and uric acid. As these pass through the nephron, the urine becomes more concentrated. The uric acid and calcium may be deposited at the top of the ureter, forming a stone.

Can you live with only one kidney?

Yes, many people do. If one kidney is diseased or damaged, it can be removed, and the other kidney will do the job of two. Some people who have both kidneys damaged or diseased need a kidney transplant. A healthy kidney from a donor is plumbed into their blood circulation and takes over the job of their own kidneys.

How does a kidney machine work?

A kidney machine filters blood by a process called dialysis. A tube inserted into an artery in a patient's arm or leg carries blood to the machine, where it is pumped through cellophane tubing in a container of liquid. Wastes in the blood pass through the walls of the tubing into the liquid, and substances that the body needs pass from the liquid into the blood. The clean blood is returned to the patient through a tube connected to a vein in his arm or leg.

Kidney dialysis filters wastes from the blood if the kidneys fail. The blood must pass through the machine 20 times before it is cleaned properly.

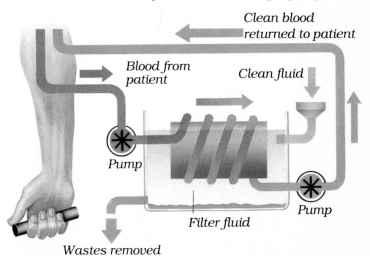

Clean blood returned to patient

Blood from patient

Clean fluid

Pump

Pump

Filter fluid

Wastes removed

43

SKIN and HAIR

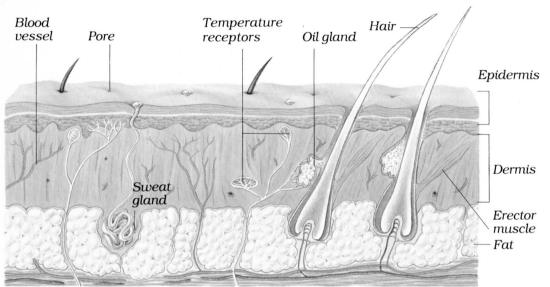

Blood vessel Pore Temperature receptors Oil gland Hair Epidermis Dermis Erector muscle Fat Sweat gland

There are two main layers to the skin. The outer, protective layer is called the epidermis. Underneath the epidermis is the dermis. It contains nerves, sensory receptors that can detect pressure and temperature; blood vessels; hair roots; and glands.

Why do we have skin?

Skin is a waterproof, flexible covering that protects us from the outside world and helps keep out harmful germs. Our skin is sensitive to touch, heat, cold, and pain. It allows us to sense what is happening around us. Skin helps protect us from harmful rays in strong sunlight and uses some sunlight to make vitamin D. Skin also helps control our body temperature.

How many layers does skin have?

Skin has two main layers: an outer, protective layer, called the epidermis, and a thicker layer beneath it called the dermis. The dermis contains nerves, sense organs, blood vessels, hair roots, oil glands, and sweat glands. Below the dermis is a layer of fat that helps keep the body warm and acts as an energy supply.

Where is new skin produced?

New skin is produced at the base of the epidermis. Here, skin cells are continually splitting to produce new cells. The new cells push the older cells upward, toward the surface of the skin. This takes about three or four weeks. By the time the skin cells reach the surface they are dead and have been squeezed flat. Dead cells on the surface are continually scraped off and replaced by new cells from underneath.

What makes skin so tough?

A flexible substance called keratin makes skin cells hard and germ-proof so that they can provide a tough covering for the body. As new skin cells move up through the layers of the epidermis they are filled with keratin. Fibers of an elastic protein in the dermis give the skin its flexibility.

Why do we have oil glands in our skin?

The oil glands in our skin produce an oily fluid called sebum. Sebum coats our skin and hair and keeps them supple. It also contains chemicals that kill germs.

Is skin really waterproof?

Yes. Sebum helps keep the skin waterproof. If you stay in the bath for too long, this waterproof coat eventually is washed away. Water soaks into your epidermis cells, causing them to pucker up into wrinkles. Once you get out of the water your skin returns to normal.

Why does skin need to be waterproof?

Skin needs to be waterproof to protect the tissues underneath it and to make sure that the fluids inside our body do not escape.

If water seeps past the skin's oily coating, it eventually makes the skin swell and wrinkle.

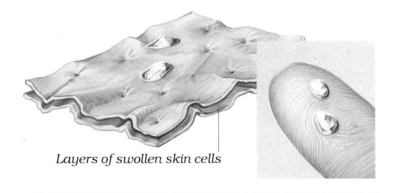

Layers of swollen skin cells

How does our skin cool us down?

When we get too hot we sweat more. As the sweat evaporates it cools us down. At the same time, tiny blood vessels in our dermis widen and bring more warm blood to the skin's surface. Some of the heat is lost into the surrounding air.

How does our skin keep us warm?

When we get cold the blood vessels in the dermis narrow so that less heat is brought to the surface of the skin. Fine hairs on our skin stand on end, helping to trap a layer of warm air next to our bodies.

The color of someone's skin depends on the amount of pigment it contains.

What is melanin?

Melanin is a dark-brown substance, or pigment, in the skin. It is produced by special cells, or melanocytes, at the base of the epidermis. Melanin protects the skin from the sun's harmful ultraviolet rays.

Why are people's skins different colors?

The color of your skin depends on how much melanin there is in the epidermis. In a black person's skin there is a lot of melanin. In a white person's skin there is less melanin, and the small blood vessels close to the surface of the dermis give the skin its pink color. People with yellowish skin have larger amounts of a pigment called carotene.

What is sweat made of?

Sweat is a salt-water liquid that contains small amounts of the body's waste substances. On an extremely hot day the body may lose up to 10 quarts of sweat, which contains about 1 ounce of salt.

Where does sweat come from?

Sweat is produced by glands in the dermis and is released onto the skin through tiny openings called pores. There are many sweat glands under the arms, in the groin, and on the hands, feet, and face.

What is a bruise?

A bruise is a purplish mark that appears when tiny blood vessels in the skin break, usually after a hard knock. Because our skin is tougher than the tissues beneath it, it is possible to damage the blood vessels without breaking the skin itself. Blood leaks out from the blood vessels into the surrounding tissues and makes them turn dark. A bruise is often painful and swollen as well.

Why do bruises change color?

Bruises are first dark purple, then change through blue, green, and yellow before fading away altogether. These color changes are a result of the blood being broken down and reabsorbed. The blood pigment hemoglobin is first purple-blue, because it has no oxygen. Later, the blood is gradually broken down to green and yellow pigments before being fully reabsorbed by the body.

How does skin heal itself?

Cut or injured skin can heal itself automatically. If someone cuts herself and starts to bleed, the blood soon forms a clot that stops further bleeding. The clot dries to form a scab, which prevents germs from entering the damaged skin. Beneath the scab, new skin cells grow across the wound. When the skin is healed the scab drops off.

Though the skin produces melanin to darken and protect the skin, strong sunlight is dangerous, and overexposure can lead to skin cancer.

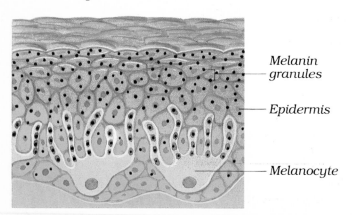

Melanin granules

Epidermis

Melanocyte

A bruise is caused by blood from broken vessels beneath the skin leaking into nearby tissues.

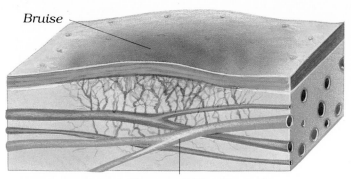

Bruise

Damaged blood vessels

Why does skin become wrinkled?

Skin wrinkles because it fits the body less tightly as we get older. When we are young, our skin is very elastic and bounces back into place after stretching. As we get older, the skin becomes drier, thinner, and less elastic. This leads to wrinkles and folds.

How thick is a layer of skin?

Skin varies in thickness according to how flexible it needs to be and how much physical protection it has to provide. In your eyelids the skin is only about 0.02 inch thick, while over most of your body it is 0.08 inch thick. The palms of your hand are up to 0.12 inch thick, and the soles of your feet up to a quarter inch thick.

What are goose pimples?

Goose pimples are the tiny bumps on the skin that appear when we get cold. When the temperature drops the hairs on our body stand on end. This traps a layer of warm air next to the skin. The tiny muscles that pull the hairs upright also cause our skin to bunch up, forming a bump.

How does skin tan?

In strong sunlight, the skin produces extra melanin to protect it from harmful ultraviolet rays. This melanin spreads through the epidermis in the form of tiny black grains. Eventually the skin turns darker, producing a tan. Every skin color turns darker with exposure to sunlight.

How much skin do we have?

If a child of eight could remove his or her skin and spread it out, it would cover an area of nearly 2 square yards and weigh about 6.5 pounds. On average, an adult has about 2.4 square yards of skin, weighing about 9 pounds.

Why do we have fingernails?

We have fingernails to provide a firm support for the skin to press against when we handle or touch objects. Fingernails also allow us to do some delicate things, like untie knots.

What are nails made of?

Nails are made of dead cells that contain keratin, the protein found in the outer layer of skin. Nails grow by being pushed out of a pit in the skin called the nailbed, which lies horizontal to the skin. As the nail grows it slides along the surface of the nailbed to the fingertip. Most of the nail is pink, because the blood vessels underneath it show through.

How quickly do nails grow?

Nails grow at the rate of about 0.004 inch a day, which adds up to about 0.12 inch a month. Nails are dead and have no nerve endings in them, so cutting them does not hurt.

The white "half-moon" at the base of the nail is the lunula. Underneath this is a layer of cells from which the nail grows.

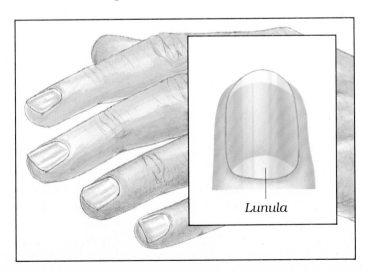

Lunula

What causes acne?

Teenagers often suffer from acne—pimples on the skin. The skin's oil, sebum, is produced in larger quantities during adolescence. The extra sebum sometimes blocks oil glands and the glands may become infected, causing pimples.

Fingerprints

Arch   *Loop*

Whorl   *Composite*

Some common fingerprint patterns are shown here. You can take your own prints by pressing your fingers onto an inkpad and then onto a clean sheet of paper.

Are any two fingerprints the same?

No. Even identical twins have different fingerprints. The print itself is caused by a pattern of ridges in the dermis. Even if the epidermis is damaged, the fingerprint is not altered.

What is an albino?

An albino is someone whose skin contains no melanin. This means they have white hair, milky-white or bright-pink skin, and pinkish eyes. Albinos are very sensitive to sunlight, because without melanin their skin cannot tan.

What happens when you blush?

Blushing is a nervous reaction that triggers the tiny blood vessels in your skin to widen. This allows more blood to flow to your skin and creates the reddening effect.

What is a freckle?

A freckle is a tiny patch of light brown skin that contains extra melanin. Freckles are harmless. They appear mostly on the face and arms.

Hair

What are the parts of a hair?

Hair has two parts, the shaft and the root. The root is embedded in the dermis of the skin and is enclosed in a tiny pit called a hair follicle. The shaft contains the pigment that gives hair its color.

What is hair for?

Hair helps to prevent heat loss from the body, because it is able to trap a layer of warm air next to the skin. Hair is particularly useful on top of the head—otherwise we would lose a lot of heat through our heads. Head hair also protects the scalp from the burning rays of the sun. Hair in the nostrils helps keep our lungs clean by filtering out particles of dust and dirt in the air we breathe in.

Why is hair different colors?

Hair color is determined by the mixture of pigments that it contains. Hair-producing cells can produce a mixture of black, red, and yellow pigments. For example, dark-haired people have mostly black pigment and fair-haired people have mostly yellow pigment.

What makes hair curly?

Hair is curly, wavy, or straight depending on the shape of the follicles it grows from. Straight hair grows from round follicles, wavy hair from oval follicles, and curly hair from flat follicles.

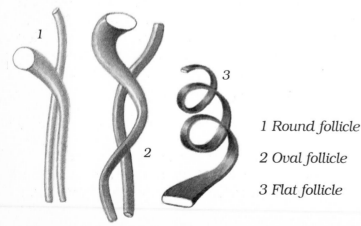

1 Round follicle

2 Oval follicle

3 Flat follicle

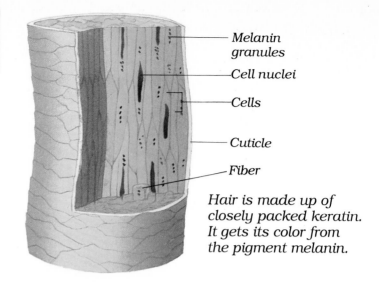

Melanin granules

Cell nuclei

Cells

Cuticle

Fiber

Hair is made up of closely packed keratin. It gets its color from the pigment melanin.

What is hair made of?

Hair is made of keratin, the same substance found in nails and skin. Hair itself is not alive, but is made by living cells in the hair follicles. New cells produced in the follicles push older cells upward, which makes hair grow longer.

Who had the longest hair?

The record for the longest hair goes to a monk called Swami Pandarasannadhi, from Madras in India. When he died, his hair measured nearly 10 yards in length!

Why does hair go gray?

Hair goes gray because as we get older, some hairs lack pigment. The resulting mixture of white and colored hair gives a gray appearance. When all the hairs have lost all their pigment, the hair looks white. The tendency to go gray is a family trait. Some people go gray sooner than others.

How strong is hair?

Hair is extremely strong. The average adult could be lifted by a rope made from about a thousand human hairs.

How many hairs do we have?

Most people have about 100,000 hairs on their head alone.

What is alopecia?

Alopecia is a condition in which the hair falls out in patches. There may be no obvious reason for this, although it is sometimes caused by certain types of medication. Occasionally people who feel under stress or who have recently had a bad shock develop alopecia. Usually the hair grows back again on its own.

Why do we have eyelashes?

Eyelashes act as protection for our eyes. Our eyelashes help stop dust and other particles from reaching the delicate surface of the eye and irritating it. Our eyebrows, however, are probably used to make signals, as a means of nonverbal communication, rather than as protection for our eyes.

Why do men have beards?

At puberty, the fine hair on boys' chins and upper lips becomes thicker. If they do not shave, a beard and mustache will grow. This is because the male hormone, testosterone, activates hair follicles on the face.

What is a boil?

A boil is a blocked hair follicle that has become infected with germs. White blood cells attack the infection and the area becomes tender. Some white or yellow pus forms a head on the boil.

What are nits?

Nits are the eggs of head lice. You can catch lice by coming into direct contact with a person who has them, or by sharing a hat or comb with someone who has them. A special shampoo can be used to get rid of both eggs and lice.

How fast does hair grow?

Hair grows at a rate of about 0.4 inch a month. A hair can keep growing for roughly six years and may reach a length of over three feet. Generally, the hair then falls out and another hair starts to grow in its place. In this way, the average person loses 50 to 100 hairs a day, but these are continuously replaced.

Why do some men go bald?

In some men testosterone seems to affect the hair follicles, slowing down or switching off hair growth, so that lost hair is not replaced. But bald men do not lose their hair altogether; it is replaced by short, very fine hair, which is visible only close up. Baldness seems to run in families.

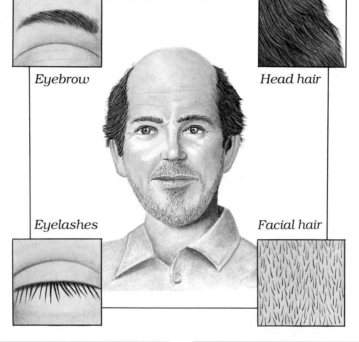

Eyebrow

Head hair

Eyelashes

Facial hair

We have hair over most of our bodies, but it is most obvious in a few places. On our heads we have hair to protect our scalp, eyebrows, and eyelashes to protect our eyes. A man also has hair on his chin and upper lip which, if he does not shave, will grow into a beard and mustache.

What is dandruff?

Dandruff is dead skin that flakes off the scalp. It can be caused by the scalp making too little or too much sebum. It can be treated by washing your hair regularly with a medicated shampoo.

Which animals live in our hair?

As you sit reading this, tiny creatures called follicle mites are crawling over your hair, eyebrows, and eyelashes. They are harmless and everyone has them. They live in the hair follicles and oil glands, and feed on dead skin cells.

NERVES and SENSES

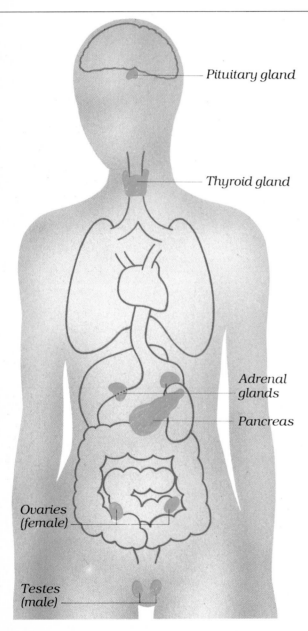

— Pituitary gland

— Thyroid gland

Adrenal
glands

— Pancreas

Ovaries
(female)

Testes
(male)

The endocrine glands help coordinate the body's activities by releasing chemical messengers called hormones into the bloodstream.

What is coordination?

Coordination is the way different activities in the body are linked together. For example, heart rate and breathing are not totally separate. When you exercise, your breathing rate and heart rate go up at the same time so that oxygen is delivered more quickly to your muscles.

How are the body's actions coordinated?

The body relies on two systems to coordinate its actions. The nervous system sends messages to and from the brain as electrical signals along nerves. The hormonal (endocrine) system sends chemical messengers called hormones around the body through the bloodstream.

What are hormones?

Hormones are chemicals produced in one part of the body that have an effect on another part. For example, the hormone insulin is produced by the pancreas and affects the functioning of the liver and other tissues in the body.

How many hormones are there?

There are over 30 hormones. They are produced by structures called endocrine glands that are found in the head, neck, and torso.

Which processes do hormones affect?

Hormones have an enormous effect on many processes, from our growth to the workings of our reproduction system. Hormones also help with controlling digestion, the production of urine, and the general activity of the body.

How do hormones affect growth?

Height is controlled by a growth hormone produced by the pituitary gland. Too much can make a person very tall, and too little can stunt their growth. Today, children with abnormal levels can be treated so that they grow to a more average size.

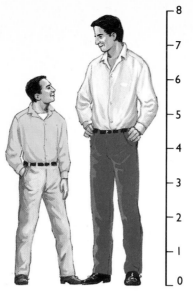

Height (feet)

Overproduction of growth hormone causes people to grow above average height.

Which is the most important gland?

The pituitary gland is the most important, because it produces hormones that control most of the other endocrine glands.

Can hormones make you overactive?

Yes. The main hormone that affects how active you are is thyroxine. It is produced by the thyroid gland in the neck. Thyroxine controls how quickly the cells in your body convert food to energy. Too much thyroxine can make people thin and overactive.

What does insulin do?

Insulin controls how much glucose (sugar) there is in the blood. After a meal, the level of glucose rises, because glucose is produced from digested food. Insulin is then released to make sure the glucose level does not get too high.

How does insulin work?

After a meal, insulin causes the liver to convert glucose to a type of starch (called glycogen) and store it for future use. When the blood glucose level falls, the pancreas produces less insulin and the stored glucose is released so it can be used by the body to produce energy.

What is diabetes?

Diabetes is a condition in which people do not produce the right amounts of insulin. As a result, they cannot control their blood glucose level. After a meal the glucose level may rise too much, causing glucose to collect in the urine. At other times, the glucose level may fall too low, and the person may lose consciousness because the brain is not getting enough glucose.

How is diabetes treated?

Diabetes can be controlled by a combination of insulin injections or tablets and a careful diet.

What is the "fight or flight" response?

When you are frightened or excited, the adrenal glands release a hormone called adrenaline, which prepares your body for action. Your heartbeat and breathing speed up, and more blood is sent to the muscles in your arms and legs. This reaction is called the "fight or flight" response. It prepares you for standing your ground and fighting—or fleeing quickly.

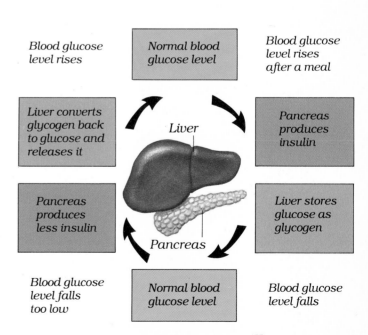

The liver controls the level of glucose in the bloodstream under the influence of the hormone insulin, which is produced by the pancreas.

The Nervous System

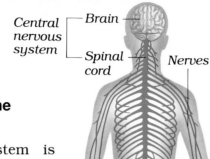

Central nervous system — Brain

Spinal cord

Nerves

What makes up the nervous system?

The nervous system is made up of millions of nerve cells, which carry tiny electrical messages around the body. It has two main parts: the central nervous system (CNS), made up of the brain and spinal cord; and the peripheral nervous system (PNS), made up of all the nerves that run from the CNS.

The nervous system is a communication network for the body. It helps all its parts work together effectively.

Where is the spinal cord?

The spinal cord runs from the base of your brain to the lower part of your back. It is a column of nervous tissue that acts like a relay station. It connects the brain with the nerves that run to other parts of your body, from your neck down to your toes. The spinal cord weighs less than an ounce. For protection, it is encased in a series of bones called vertebrae, which make up the spine.

How many nerves do you have?

Running between your brain and the sense organs and muscles in your head are 24 large nerves—the cranial nerves. These include nerves from your eyes, nose, and ears. Sixty-two more nerves, the spinal nerves, run from your spinal cord to the rest of the body.

What do nerve cells look like?

All nerve cells, or neurons, have a fat cell body that contains the nucleus. Leading out of the cell body is a long fiber called the axon. Branches at the end of the axon deliver messages to the next cell. Nerve cells also have many shorter branches called dendrites, which pick up messages from other nerve cells.

Are all nerve cells the same?

No, there are three types of nerve cells: motor, sensory, and connector nerve cells. They vary in shape, location, and the job they do.

What do motor nerve cells do?

Motor nerve cells carry messages from the brain and spinal cord (the central nervous system) to muscles and glands around the body.

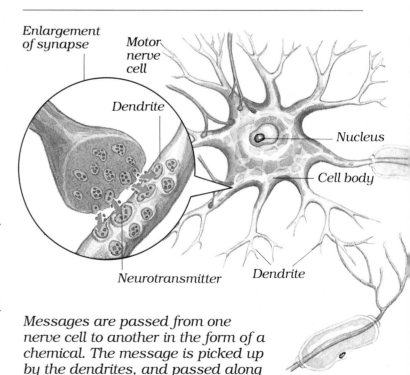

Enlargement of synapse

Motor nerve cell

Dendrite

Nucleus

Cell body

Neurotransmitter

Dendrite

Messages are passed from one nerve cell to another in the form of a chemical. The message is picked up by the dendrites, and passed along the axon as an electrical signal.

How does a message travel along a nerve?

A message is picked up by a nerve cell at its dendrite end. The message travels through the cell as a small electrical current called a nerve impulse. When the message gets to the end of the axon it is passed on to the next cell.

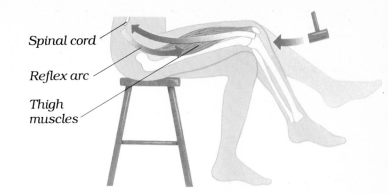

Being tapped on the knee while sitting cross-legged will cause a reflex "knee-jerk" reaction.

How is a message passed from one nerve cell to the next?

One nerve cell does not actually touch the next. There is a slight gap, called a synapse, between them. The message hops across this gap, not as an electric current, but as a chemical. The branched ends of axons have little knobs on them. When triggered by a nerve impulse, these knobs release a chemical called a neurotransmitter, which passes across the gap. This stimulates the cell next door, setting up a new nerve impulse so that the message continues.

How fast do messages travel along nerves?

A nerve impulse can travel along a nerve fiber at 220 miles an hour, or 330 feet a second, but it is slowed down when it has to jump across a synapse.

What do sensory nerve cells do?

Sensory nerve cells connect the body's sense organs with the central nervous system. It is through these cells that information from sense organs, such as your eyes, reaches your brain.

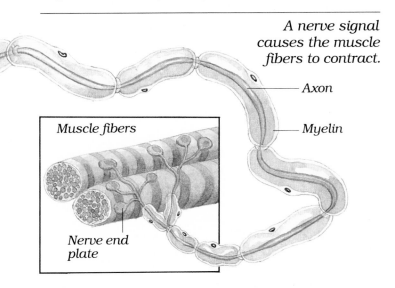

A nerve signal causes the muscle fibers to contract.

Axon

Myelin

Muscle fibers

Nerve end plate

Where do you find connector nerve cells?

You find these in the brain and spinal cord. Connector nerve cells link up sensory nerve cells with motor nerve cells and allow you to make decisions.

What is a reflex?

When you react to something without thinking, your action is called a reflex. For example, if your hand touches something hot, you will jerk it away without stopping to think about it. Most reflexes are controlled by your spinal cord and hardly involve your brain at all.

What causes a reflex?

A reflex is caused by a simple circuit of nerve cells called a reflex arc. Most reflex arcs have five parts. A sensory receptor, such as a nerve ending in your finger, detects the heat (the stimulus). A sensory nerve cell carries the message to the spinal cord, and a connector nerve cell then delivers it across the spinal cord to a motor nerve cell. This carries a return signal from the spinal cord to your muscles, which move your hand away from the hot object.

Why are reflexes useful?

Reflexes are useful because they protect you from danger. If a small object moves toward your eye, you blink automatically. A reflex reaction is far quicker than a response produced by the brain. Having reflexes also means that your conscious mind does not have to be constantly alert to all possible dangers.

Are nerves insulated?

Yes. Most nerve fibers are wrapped in a fatty substance called myelin, which helps keep electrical messages from escaping.

The Senses

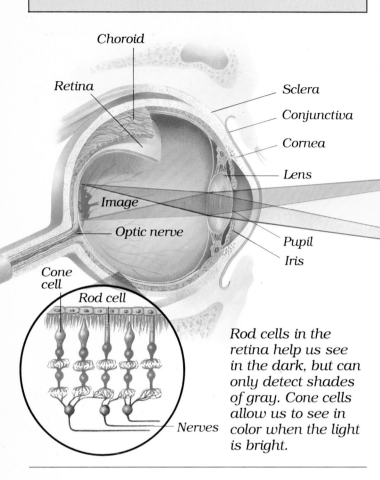

Choroid

Retina

Sclera

Conjunctiva

Cornea

Lens

Image

Optic nerve

Pupil

Iris

Cone cell

Rod cell

Object

Light rays

The eye sees upside down, but the brain corrects the image.

Rod cells in the retina help us see in the dark, but can only detect shades of gray. Cone cells allow us to see in color when the light is bright.

Nerves

What are your five senses?

Your five senses are sight, hearing, smell, taste, and touch.

What is a stimulus?

A stimulus (plural, stimuli) is anything that produces a response in the body. The main stimuli in our surroundings are light, sound, heat, cold, touch, pressure, and chemicals.

How do our senses work?

Our sense organs, such as our eyes, contain special cells called sensory receptors. These cells pass information about the outside world to nerve cells, which then transmit a message to the brain. Sensory receptors in the eye receive information in the form of light rays. Those in taste buds detect chemicals in food.

What are eyes made of?

The eyes are two tough balls of tissue containing transparent jelly. At the front of each eye is a transparent covering called the cornea. The colored part of the eye is called the iris. It surrounds the pupil, a dark hole through which light enters the eyeball. Six muscles connect the eyeball to the bones in the eye socket and allow the eyeball to move around. The optic nerve runs out of the back of the eye and goes to the brain.

How do our eyes work?

Light rays from an outside scene enter the eyes and pass through the pupil to the lens. Both the curved surface of the eye and the lens bend the rays and focus them into a clear image on the retina—a layer of light-sensitive cells at the back of the eye. Cells in the retina send messages along the optic nerve to the brain.

Why does the brain flip the image?

The image formed on your retina is upside down because of the way the lens bends light rays. The brain automatically turns the image right side up before you "see" it.

How is the eye like a camera?

Both a camera and the eye can control the amount of light that enters them. Both have a lens to focus the image, and both register the image on a light-sensitive surface—photographic film in the camera, and the retina in the eye.

What gives your eyes their color?

Your eye color is produced by a pigment called melanin. Eyes can be brown, blue, gray, green, or somewhere in between. The color depends on how much melanin is present in the iris—brown eyes contain much more than blue eyes.

What is the retina made of?

The retina contains about 125 million light-sensitive cells called rods and about 7 million cells called cones. The rods detect the brightness of the light shining on them. The cones detect the color of the light.

How do we see colors?

There are three types of cone cell, each sensitive to one of three colors: red, blue, or green. We see other colors when a combination of cone cells are triggered. For example, when both red and green cones are stimulated in equal amounts, the brain interprets the signals as the color yellow.

Can we see color in dim light?

No. In dim light only the rod cells are triggered. These are sensitive to the amount of light, but not its color. If a flashlight is used to bathe part of the dimly lit area in bright light, the color-sensitive cells (the cones) can operate and we are able to see colors.

Why do our pupils change size?

Our pupils change size to allow more or less light into our eyes. In bright light, muscles around the pupil contract so that it grows small. This prevents too much light from damaging the eye. In dim light, different muscles contract and the pupil grows larger to let in more light.

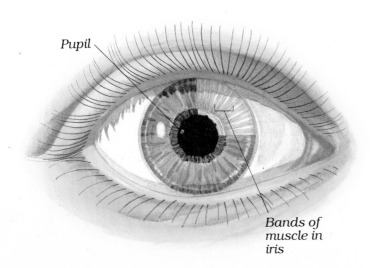

Pupil

Bands of muscle in iris

What is color blindness?

Someone who is color-blind cannot see the full range of colors—some appear gray. The most common form is red-green color blindness, where a person's red- or green-sensitive cone cells do not work properly. They have difficulty in distinguishing reds, greens, and browns. This affects about 1 in 12 men. The condition is far less common in women.

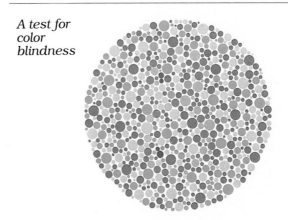

A test for color blindness

Is there a test for color blindness?

Color blindness is detected by using special charts, containing patterns made up of colored dots. Someone who is color-blind could not make out the pattern shown above.

How many colors can we see?

The human eye is so sensitive that, under the best conditions, it is able to detect 10 million different color shades.

When the light is too bright, muscles in the iris automatically reduce the size of the pupil to protect the sensitive retina.

Never look directly at the Sun

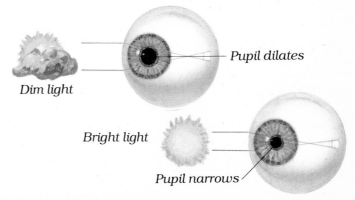

Dim light

Pupil dilates

Bright light

Pupil narrows

What is our field of vision?

Our eyes cover an angle of about 200 degrees (just over a semicircle). This is called our field of vision. We can see in three dimensions over an angle of nearly 140 degrees. This is the area where the fields of vision of the right and left eyes overlap.

Why are two eyes better than one?

There are three main advantages in having two eyes. First, two eyes can see over a larger area than just one. Also, because our eyes are about 2.5 inches apart, they see objects from slightly different angles. The brain fits these two images together to give us a three-dimensional (3-D) picture. Finally, having 3-D vision also helps us to judge distances.

Right field of view

Left field of view

Field of 3-D vision

Our two eyes work together to help our brain judge the distance and depth of an object.

What makes our eyes water?

Crying makes our eyes water when we are upset, or our eyes may water to wash away dirt or an irritation, such as smoke. Normally, tear fluid drains away at roughly the same rate that it is produced. However, if tear fluid forms more quickly than it is drained away, it wells up, forming tears.

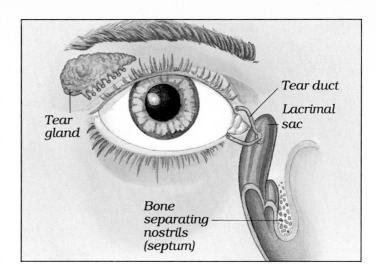

Tear gland

Tear duct

Lacrimal sac

Bone separating nostrils (septum)

The tear glands produce tears at the same rate that the tear ducts drain them away.

What keeps our eyes shiny?

Tear fluid keeps our eyes shiny and moist. It is produced all the time by a special gland just above the eyeball. Tear fluid contains a chemical that kills germs. It also contains food and oxygen, which the cornea needs to stay alive. Tear fluid drains away down a tiny tear duct in the corner of each eye and eventually empties into the nose.

Why do we blink?

We blink to help protect our eyes. Every time we blink our eyelids act like windshield wipers, spreading tear fluid over our eyes to keep them clean and moist. We blink automatically if something gets near to our eyes, or if dirt gets inside and irritates them.

How often do we blink?

We blink on average about six times a minute. This adds up to almost a year in a lifetime! We blink less often when we are concentrating and more often when we are tired.

How is eyesight tested?

An eye specialist, or optician, tests the sharpness of someone's vision by asking them to read eight rows of letters on an eye chart. The optician can also examine the back of the eye to check for eye disorders.

Why do some people need glasses?

People need glasses if the lenses in their eyes cannot focus the light rays properly on the retina. The image they see looks fuzzy. Wearing glasses can help correct their sight.

How do we focus?

To form a clear image of something (to focus), our eyes must be able to bend light rays from the object so that they fall directly on the retina. We can focus on objects at different distances because the lenses in our eyes can change shape. They become rounder when we look at a near object and flatter when we look at something farther away.

Nearsightedness

For a nearsighted person, the prices at the flower stall would be a blur.

What can a nearsighted person see?

To a nearsighted person only near objects are clear. Distant objects look fuzzy because they are focused in front of the retina. Nearsighted people wear glasses with concave lenses. These bend light rays slightly outward so that they focus on the retina, rather than in front of it.

Is eating carrots good for your eyesight?

Surprisingly, it can be. Carrots contain a lot of vitamin A, which is used to make one of the pigments in the light-sensitive cells of the eye. Eating lots of carrots can help improve very poor night vision.

How do contact lenses work?

Contact lenses are thin plastic disks that rest on the surface of the eye and act like the lenses in glasses. Contact lenses can be hard or soft. Soft lenses absorb water from the tear fluid, but hard lenses do not. Soft lenses are easier to get used to and can be worn for longer, but they are much more expensive and more fragile.

What are reading glasses?

As some people get older, their lenses harden slightly and do not fatten properly for close-focusing. For close-up work, such as reading, they need glasses that have converging lenses to bend the light rays onto the retina.

Farsightedness

But a farsighted person would find the prices at the flower stall easy to read.

What makes people farsighted?

A common cause of farsightedness is that the eyeball is too short from front to back. Light rays from near objects are focused behind the retina and so they look blurred. Only distant objects are clear. Glasses with convex lenses, which bend light rays inward slightly, can help.

Why does "sleep" collect in our eyes?

When we are asleep, our eyes still blink, although more slowly. Our eyeballs still move around. As tear fluid moves across the eye, dust and mucus sometimes collect in the corner, and we call this "sleep."

O

X

To find your blind spot, close your left eye and look at the O. Hold the book at arm's length and then bring it toward you until the X disappears.

Where is the blind spot?

The blind spot is the place at the back of the eye where the optic nerve leaves the eyeball. There are no light-sensitive cells here, so it produces a blank spot in our field of vision. We do not normally notice our blind spots, because one eye compensates for the other.

Where is the fovea?

The fovea is a shallow dip in the retina, opposite the pupil. It contains the most receptor cells and so is the area of sharpest vision. People with normal vision focus light rays from a distant object precisely onto the fovea.

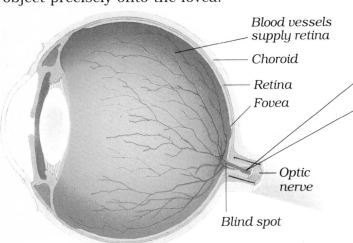

Blood vessels supply retina

Choroid

Retina

Fovea

Optic nerve

Blind spot

Can someone be right-eyed as well as right-handed?

Yes. We all have one eye that we use more than the other. To find out which eye you use most, hold a pencil at arm's length and line it up with a distant object. Close one eye and then open it again. Repeat this with the other eye. Closing one of your eyes will make the pencil jump to one side. The closed eye is your dominant eye—the one you use most.

What is the choroid?

The choroid is a pigmented layer between the white of the eye (the sclera) and the retina. The pigment absorbs light from the retina and stops it from passing through the back of the eye. The pigment also gives the eye its color.

How fast does a message get from your eye to your brain?

When light hits your retina, the message travels to the brain at about 300 miles an hour. An image is formed in the brain about two-thousandths of a second later.

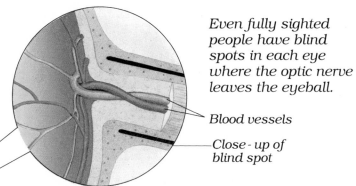

Even fully sighted people have blind spots in each eye where the optic nerve leaves the eyeball.

Blood vessels

Close-up of blind spot

Are babies born with full eyesight?

Newborn babies can see only light and shadow. Their eyesight gradually improves with use. Young babies need to hold objects at arm's length to see them properly. It takes several months for the two eyes to coordinate and move together. Vision keeps improving until about the age of eight.

What is astigmatism?

People with astigmatism have slightly blurred vision because the cornea of their eye is uneven. Some light rays are bent more than others and are not clearly focused on the retina. Astigmatism usually can be corrected by wearing specially prepared lenses.

What is a detached retina?

As some people get older, part of the retina lifts away from the layer underneath. This can cause blurred vision, flashes of light, and partial loss of sight. The part of the retina that is lifting away can sometimes be sealed down again using special laser or freezing techniques.

What is 20/20 vision?

If you have 20/20 vision you have perfect eyesight. The numbers refer to distances from an eye-test wall chart. A reading of 20/20 means that the lowest row of letters the person is able to read at a distance of 20 feet is the same one that someone with normal vision can read at 20 feet. Someone with 20/40 vision cannot see so well. At 20 feet that person is only able to read a row of letters that someone with normal sight can read at 40 feet. In most countries the distances are in meters, so 20/20 vision is called 6/6 vision.

Do blind people dream?

Yes. But people blind from birth use their other senses—touch, sound, even smell and taste—when they are dreaming.

What does it mean to be cross-eyed?

Being cross-eyed means that the two eyes do not move together. It may be caused by a lazy eye muscle. One eye wanders so that each eye looks in a slightly different direction. As a result, the brain receives two different images. In order to make sense of them, it ignores the signals from one eye. If the problem is not treated early, this eye becomes useless. Wearing a patch over the good eye can encourage the lazy one to work harder, and after a time the condition usually corrects itself.

What are the "specks" you see when you look at a bright light?

These specks are cells and cell fragments that are shed into the fluid of the eye. They float over the surface of the eye and do not do any harm. Normally you do not notice them.

What is a cataract?

A cataract is a condition of the eye in which the lens becomes cloudy. The faulty lens is sometimes removed and replaced with a plastic one. Glasses with strong corrective lenses may also be needed.

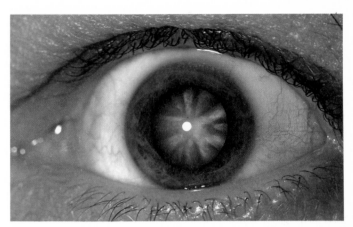

Most cataracts develop over a number of years and are a result of growing older. They are especially common in countries where nutrition is poor.

What is glaucoma?

Glaucoma is a condition in which the jellylike fluid in the eyeball is produced faster than it drains away. Pressure builds up inside the eye and presses against the retina. Blood vessels and nerve cells are damaged, which can cause blindness. Eye drops or special tablets can stop the fluid from being formed so quickly, but sometimes an operation is needed to drain the fluid away.

What causes a sty?

A sty occurs when an oil gland at the base of an eyelash becomes infected by bacteria. Normally it is cured by removing the eyelash and bathing the eye in hot water.

What is conjunctivitis?

Conjunctivitis, or "pink-eye," is an infection or irritation of the conjunctiva, the delicate membrane that covers the front of the eye. It can make your eyes sticky, red, and painful. Conjunctivitis can often be treated with antibiotics.

Hearing

Why do we have an ear flap?

The ear flap, or pinna, is the part of the ear we can see. It helps funnel sounds down into our ear canal and to the inner workings of the ear. The ear flap is made of folds of skin and cartilage. It is folded so that it will spring back into shape if it is bent or squashed.

The ear not only picks up sound but also helps us keep our balance.

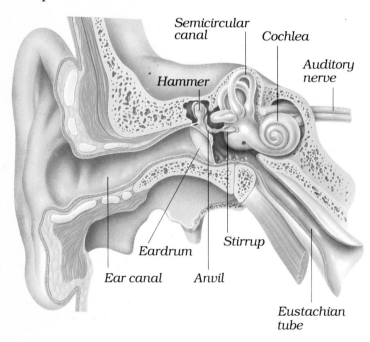

Semicircular canal

Cochlea

Auditory nerve

Hammer

Eardrum

Stirrup

Ear canal

Anvil

Eustachian tube

Where does the ear hole go to?

Most of the ear is inside the skull. The ear hole, or canal, leads to the eardrum, a membrane stretched tightly across the end of the ear canal.

What is beyond the eardrum?

Beyond the eardrum is the middle ear, which contains three tiny bones. These are called the hammer, the anvil, and the stirrup because of their shapes. Beyond that is the inner ear. This contains a fluid-filled spiral structure called the cochlea and three semicircular canals. All three parts of the ear—the outer, middle, and inner—help us hear.

How do our ears hear?

Sound is made up of pressure waves, which can travel through air, liquid, and solid objects. When these waves strike the outer ear, they are funneled down the ear canal to the eardrum, which starts to vibrate. The vibrations of the eardrum are magnified by the three bones of the middle ear. The stirrup acts like a piston, transferring these vibrations to the fluid of the inner ear. As the fluid moves, it excites special hair cells in the cochlea. These hair cells send signals along the auditory nerve to the brain, which interprets the signals as sound.

Why do our ears have wax in them?

The wax in our ears is made by cells lining the ear canal. The wax contains substances that stop germs from growing in our ears. It also traps dirt and dust, which works its way out of the ear with the wax.

Why do people have their ears syringed?

If the wax in the ears gets too hard it can block the ear and cause partial deafness. Special ear drops can be used to soften the wax. The ears are then syringed with warm water to remove it.

Why do we have two ears?

By having two ears we can tell which direction sound is coming from. A sound from the right will reach the right ear first and sound slightly louder than the sound reaching the left ear.

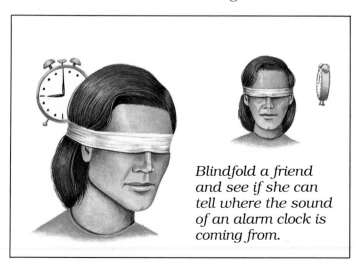

Blindfold a friend and see if she can tell where the sound of an alarm clock is coming from.

What is the range of human hearing?

We can hear from a low rumble to a high-pitched hiss. Sound waves are measured in cycles per second, or hertz (Hz). Human speech lies in the frequency range of 500 to 3,000 Hz. Most young people have a hearing range between about 40 Hz and 20,000 Hz. This range is rather small when compared with dogs (who can hear up to 50,000 Hz) and bats (over 100,000 Hz). In humans, the hearing range gets much smaller from middle age on.

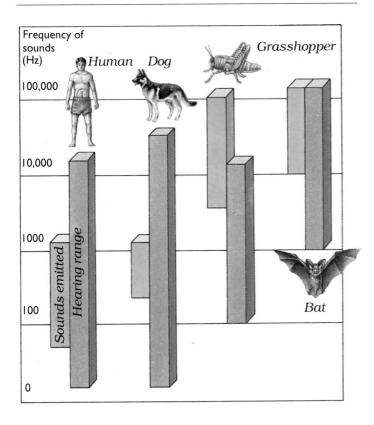

Many animals are capable of receiving sounds well beyond the range of human hearing.

Can a baby hear before it is born?

Yes. A baby's ears are partly formed only 12 weeks after it has begun to grow inside the mother's womb. After six months, it can hear the mother's breathing and heartbeat, and even sounds from outside the mother's body. The baby will be disturbed by loud noises and calmed by slow, soothing music with deep, regular bass notes.

How can the ear tell high notes from low ones?

Sound vibrations are converted in the ear to electrical signals to be sent to the brain. This happens in the coiled-up cochlea, which looks like a snail's shell. Inside the cochlea are thousands of hairlike receptor cells. The vibrations from low notes are picked up by receptors in the center of the cochlea, while high notes are detected nearer the entrance. The signals from high and low notes are sent to slightly different parts of the brain.

Can loud noises make me go deaf?

Yes, either by damaging the eardrum or the sensitive cells in the cochlea. A single loud noise, like a gunshot, can damage the eardrum temporarily. Repeated loud noise, such as amplified music, can cause permanent damage to the cells of the cochlea. Several rock musicians have gone partly deaf because of this.

What does your eustachian tube do?

The eustachian tube runs from the middle ear to the back of the throat. It lets air in and out of your middle ear so that the air pressure inside the ear is always the same as outside. If this did not happen, the eardrum would be stretched taut and would not be able to vibrate properly. You can open up the eustachian tube by swallowing, yawning, or blowing your nose.

Why do I feel deaf if I have a cold?

Sometimes, when you have a bad cold, the eustachian tube may get blocked with mucus and congestion. Air pressure can build up in the middle ear, stretching the eardrum slightly and deadening sound. This can happen with a throat infection too.

Why is it a bad idea to blow your nose too hard?

Blowing your nose too hard could force mucus and germs along the eustachian tubes and into the middle ear, where they could start a painful infection.

What causes deafness?

There are two sorts of deafness. In one type, sounds do not reach the inner ear. This could be caused by a blockage in the outer ear, such as a buildup of wax, or by an infection in the middle ear that stops the three bones from working properly. In the second type of deafness, sounds reach the inner ear, but no electrical signals are sent to the brain. Noise damage to the cochlea is one cause of this type of deafness.

How does a hearing aid work?

There are two main types of hearing aid. One works by making the sound waves reaching the ears stronger. The other type makes sound vibrations travel through the bones behind the ears to the auditory nerve. In both types of hearing aid, a microphone picks up sounds and converts them into electrical signals. These signals are then made stronger and sent to an earphone, which acts as a tiny loudspeaker. Some hearing aids are fitted with an earpiece and are worn behind the ear; others fit fully inside it.

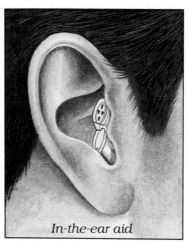

In-the-ear aid

Some hearing aids are small enough to be easily worn in the ear. Others are worn behind the ear.

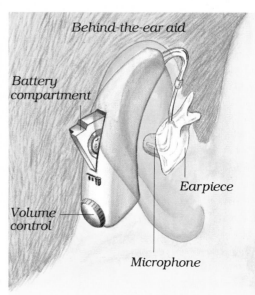

Behind-the-ear aid

Battery compartment

Earpiece

Volume control

Microphone

What is nerve deafness?

Some people are born with a damaged auditory nerve. Although their eardrum and inner ear apparatus may work perfectly, they cannot hear a thing because no signals reach their brain from the ear.

Can we hear through our bones?

Yes. Sound can travel from our mouth to our ears through our jawbones. This makes our voice sound louder and fuller to us than it does to other people. That is why a tape recording of our voice sounds so thin when we hear it played back. It also means that when we eat a crunchy food, such as celery, it makes a real racket—but to those around us it is much less noisy.

How do our ears help us balance?

Above the cochlea in the inner ear are three tiny, fluid-filled semicircular canals. These loops are our organs of balance. Each contains small pieces of chalky substance that are in contact with sensitive cells. When we move, the chalk triggers these cells to send signals to the brain. One loop detects up-and-down motion, another forward-and-backward motion, the third side-to-side motion. So whichever way we move, even if our eyes are shut, the brain is informed.

How sensitive are our ears?

The human ear can hear sounds ranging in loudness from 10 decibels to 140 decibels. A sound of 10 decibels, such as a whisper, is very quiet, while 140 decibels is painfully loud. A sound of 160 decibels, such as the lift-off of a rocket, is extremely dangerous.

What is vertigo?

Vertigo is not, as many people think, a fear of heights. It is the feeling that either you or your surroundings are spinning around. You do not have to be high up to feel it. Vertigo is a clue that there is some other problem. A common cause of vertigo is an infection in the inner ear, where the organs of balance are found.

Smell and Taste

What is the nose for?

Obviously, the nose is for smelling and for breathing. But it also cleans, warms, and moistens the air that you breathe into your lungs. The nose also makes your voice sound pleasant.

Where do the nostrils go to?

Each nostril leads back into a cavity behind the roof of the mouth, which is connected to the throat. The two nasal cavities also connect sideways to a system of spaces called the sinuses.

Why do we have sinuses?

The sinuses, eight in all, are hollow spaces in our cheekbones and around the eyes. They are connected to the nose, and help moisten the air we breathe in and give depth to our voice. The spaces also lighten the weight of our skull.

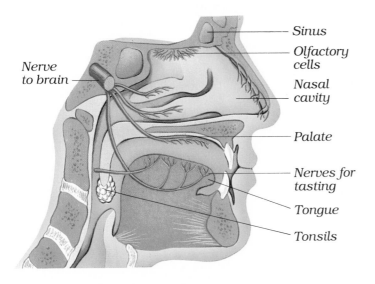

Nerve to brain — Sinus — Olfactory cells — Nasal cavity — Palate — Nerves for tasting — Tongue — Tonsils

The nerve fibers that enable us to smell things are found on the roof of the nasal cavity.

How many things can we smell?

Most people can recognize about 4,000 different scents. Someone with an extremely sensitive nose, such as a chef, wine taster, or perfume maker, can detect 10,000 different smells.

How is the nose able to smell?

On the roof of each nasal cavity is a patch of yellow-brown tissue smaller than a postage stamp. In each patch are roughly 10 million sensitive cells called olfactory cells. Each of these cells has between six and eight tiny hairs projecting from it. It is these cells that detect the chemicals that cause smells. The cells send this information to a part of the brain only 1 inch away.

Tiny hairs projecting from the olfactory cells detect the chemicals that cause smells.

Why do things smell different?

No one knows quite how the olfactory cells are able to tell one smell from another. One theory is that there are seven basic smells and that all other smells are a combination of these. The seven are: flowery, decay, peppermint, musk, ether, mothballs, and spicy. This would mean that there were seven types of olfactory cells, each reacting to a different basic smell.

What is the advantage of smell?

The sense of smell makes a great difference to our sense of taste. We cannot taste food as well when our nose is blocked. Our sense of smell also supplies information about potential dangers—of food gone bad, for example, or of smoke from a fire.

Why does our sense of smell wear off?

If we go into a room in which there is a strong smell, for example of mothballs, the odor wears off after a while, even though it would smell strongly to someone coming into the room. This may be because the particular olfactory cells that react to the smell get tired. Another reason could be that the brain shuts off or ignores the messages coming from these cells. Shutting off one smell can be useful because it allows us to concentrate on new smells.

What does our nose do while we are asleep?

If we are sleeping on our left side, the left nostril gradually fills with mucus. After a couple of hours this sends a signal to our brain for us to turn over. In this way, the nose helps make sure our muscles are exercised during the night so we do not get cramps.

Why does a cold spoil our sense of smell?

When we have a cold our nasal membranes defend themselves against the cold virus by producing large amounts of mucus. This blocks the nose and stops the chemicals in the air from reaching the sensitive olfactory cells.

Why does my nose run on a cold day?

Cold temperatures stop cilia, the thin hairs that line your nose, from working. Cilia normally push mucus to the back of the throat, where it is swallowed. In cold weather the mucus collects in the nose and finally drips out of your nostrils.

Why do we sniff to smell things?

Sniffing makes it easier to smell something, since it directs a stream of air to the top of your nose, where the olfactory cells are.

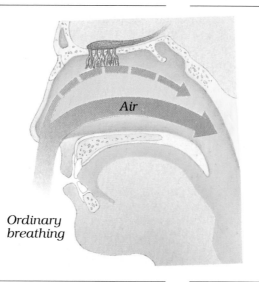

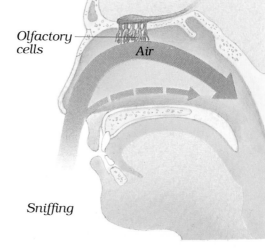

During ordinary breathing, most of the smells carried by air do not reach the olfactory cells at the top of the nose. So to smell something deeply, we draw air right up into the nasal cavity by sniffing. This stimulates the olfactory cells as much as possible and makes the smell strong.

Air

Ordinary breathing

Olfactory cells

Air

Sniffing

When does an apple taste like an onion?

An apple may taste like an onion if we confuse our sense of taste by stimulating our sense of smell at the same time. Try this out on a friend. Ask if they can tell what they are eating without looking at it. They will probably think this is easy. Cover their eyes with a blindfold. Hold a piece of onion under their nose and put a piece of apple on their tongue. What do they think they are eating? They may find it hard to tell. This experiment shows how much our sense of taste relies on our sense of smell.

What is taste?

Taste is a combination of the tongue sensing the chemicals in food and the nose smelling them. Smell is more important in tasting food.

How does the tongue taste things?

On the upper surface of the tongue are small collections of cells called taste buds. The taste-buds pick out four different tastes: bitter, sweet, sour, and salty. The way food tastes is a combination of these basic tastes.

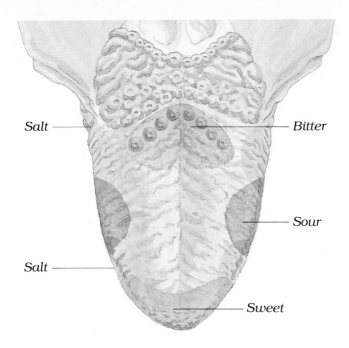

The main flavors are detected by taste buds on different parts of the tongue. Test this with cotton dipped in sugar, salt, vinegar, and coffee.

Do different parts of the mouth taste different things?

Yes. Taste buds at the tip of the tongue are good at sensing sweet things. A bit farther back, on each side of the tongue, are most of the taste buds for salty things. Farther back, at the sides of the tongue and on the roof of the mouth, are the sour-taste taste buds. Finally, right at the back of the tongue and mouth are the bitter "after-taste" taste buds.

How many taste buds do we have?

We have about 10,000 taste buds on our tongue, but they decline in number as we get older. By the age of 60 only about 65 percent of them remain. This is why our sense of taste deteriorates as we grow old.

Does food taste the same to everyone?

Just as hearing and sight vary from one person to another, so does taste. What tastes good to one person may taste horrible to another. To some extent, how things taste is learned. But it seems that our sense of taste may be partly inherited. Several chemicals show variations in human taste. The chemical sodium benzoate, for example, is sweet to some, but to others it is sour, bitter, salty, or even tasteless.

Why is hot food usually more tasty than cold?

When food is hot, it releases more chemicals into the air. These reach our olfactory cells, so the food has more taste. Our taste buds also seem to work better at warmer temperatures.

Can we tell by taste which foods are poisonous?

We can detect only some poisons by taste. Our taste buds are especially sensitive to bitter tastes. Many natural plant poisons taste very bitter, so taste can warn us against some harmful substances. But unfortunately many poisons are tasteless and some are sweet. Lead acetate tastes sweet and was used as a sweetener many years ago until it was discovered that it was a poisonous substance.

There are about 10,000 taste buds on the surface of the tongue, clustered around bumps of skin called papillae.

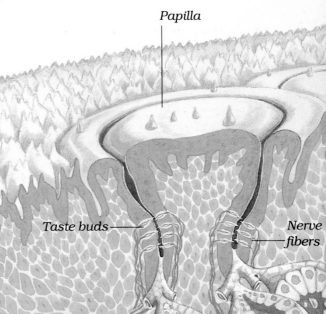

Touch

How is the skin able to sense things?

The skin has five different kinds of sensory receptors. These cells are sensitive to heat, cold, pressure, texture, and pain. The receptors are connected by sensory nerves to the spinal cord and brain. They are continuously sending signals about the state of our surroundings and what is happening on the surface of the skin.

Where are sensory receptors found?

Sensory receptors are found in different parts of the skin, depending on what they sense. Light-pressure and cold receptors are near the surface; receptors for heat and strong pressure are buried deeper.

There are more pain receptors in the skin than any other kind.

What do sensory receptors look like?

Sensory receptors are of various shapes. Pain receptors are branching, free nerve endings close to the surface of the skin. The nerve endings in other receptors are surrounded by connective tissue.

How do blind people read with their fingers?

Blind people often compensate for their lack of sight by developing other senses—hearing, smell, and touch, in particular. They may learn to read by touch using Braille, a system in which small dots raised from the surface of the paper represent letters and punctuation. Blind people can read about 100 words a minute by passing their fingertips over the page.

What causes pain?

Any stimulus that is strong enough to cause tissue damage is likely to trigger pain; for example, strong pressure, swelling, muscle spasms, or the presence or absence of certain chemicals. Other sensory receptors will also give pain signals if the stimulus they respond to is strong enough. For example, temperature receptors will give a feeling of pain if the temperature is too hot or too cold.

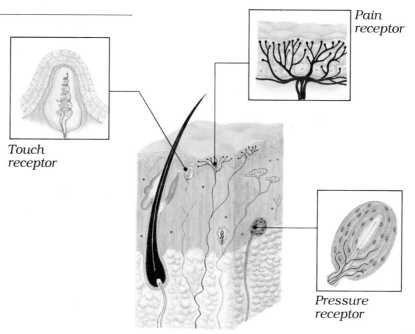

Touch receptor

Pain receptor

Pressure receptor

Why is pain useful?

Pain is useful because it tells us that something is wrong. Perhaps we have pressed our hand on something hot, or have an infection in some part of the body—either way, the pain is a warning to which we need to respond. It is there to prevent us from causing ourselves more harm.

Are there different types of pain?

Yes. Doctors talk about two main types of pain: acute and chronic. Acute pain is sharp and stabbing, and usually arrives and disappears quickly. This is the sort of pain you feel when you cut yourself. Chronic pain is a lasting pain, such as a headache. Different nerves carry the signals for the two types of pain.

How do painkillers work?

Most painkillers, or analgesics, work by blocking pain signals. These drugs stop nerve impulses from traveling across synapses either in the peripheral nervous system or in the brain and spinal cord. If the pain signals cannot reach your brain, you do not feel the pain.

Which are the most sensitive parts of the body?

The lips are most sensitive to touch and texture, while the small of the back is the least sensitive. The parts most sensitive to pressure are the fingertips, and the least sensitive is the rear end!

Why are some parts of the body more sensitive than others?

The lips and fingertips are much more sensitive than the lower back because they have more nerve endings. Our fingers and toes need to be more sensitive, since we use them to explore the world around us. A picture in which the size of the various parts of the body represents their sensitivity is shown below.

The most sensitive areas of our body are those that tell us about the world around us—our hands, tongue and lips, and feet. That is why they are so huge in this picture.

How does our skin sense heat and cold?

The sensory receptors in the skin react to a change in temperature rather than to the temperature itself. So the temperature we feel depends to an extent on what we are used to.

Put one finger in a cup of hot water and another in a cup of cold. Hold them there for a minute, then dip each finger in warm water. The finger from the hot cup will feel cold; the finger from the cold cup will feel hot.

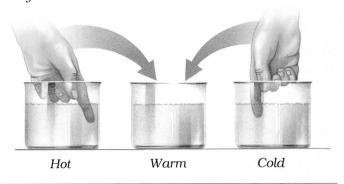

Hot   *Warm*   *Cold*

What is referred pain?

Pain is not always felt in the damaged region. When it is felt in some other part of the body instead, it is said to be "referred." For instance, a heart pain may be felt across the chest and down the left arm. A liver complaint may cause pain across the shoulders.

What causes an itch?

Little is known about the sensation of itchiness. Stimulating pain receptors can cause itching, but no nerve endings have been specifically connected with itching alone. Thinking about an itch can often bring on the urge to scratch, but the reason for this remains a mystery.

What is a phantom limb?

When someone has had a badly damaged or infected limb amputated (removed), they may afterward experience an effect known as a phantom or ghost limb. The person feels that the limb is still there, causing pain or irritation. These pains are caused by cut sensory nerves continuing to send messages to the brain. The pains usually fade with time.

REPRODUCTION and GROWTH

How are babies made?

A baby begins forming when an egg cell from the mother and a sperm cell from the father join together inside the mother's body. This is called fertilization. The fertilized egg grows and divides. If it is carried for the pregnancy's full term, the egg will become a baby.

Where do a woman's eggs come from?

Eggs are made in the ovaries, two almond-shaped organs in the woman's body. About once a month, from puberty (10 to 14 years) until the age of approximately 45 to 50, an egg is released from one of the two ovaries.

Where are the female reproductive organs?

A woman's reproductive organs are inside her lower abdomen. The womb, or uterus, is hollow with strong muscular walls. Two Fallopian tubes run out sideways from the top of the womb and curve downward. The frilly opening of each tube is wrapped around an ovary. The neck of the womb, or cervix, leads to a strong muscular tube called the vagina.

Where does fertilization take place?

The sperm fertilizes the egg in one of the woman's Fallopian tubes. The fertilized egg travels down the Fallopian tube to the womb, where the baby grows.

How big is the womb?

The womb is normally roughly the size and shape of a small pear, but it stretches during pregnancy to about 12 inches in length.

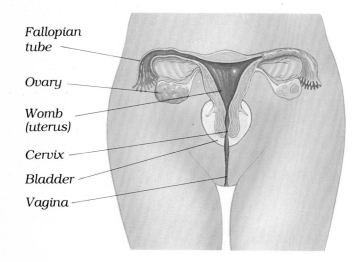

Fallopian tube

Ovary

Womb (uterus)

Cervix

Bladder

Vagina

Above: Eggs are produced in the woman's ovaries. If fertilized by sperm, the egg may develop into an embryo in the womb.

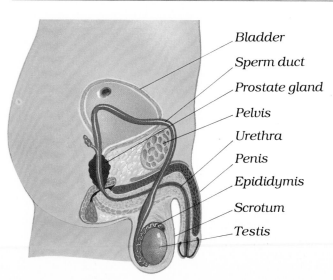

Bladder

Sperm duct

Prostate gland

Pelvis

Urethra

Penis

Epididymis

Scrotum

Testis

Right: The testes produce millions of sperm, which are released through the sperm duct.

What are the male reproductive organs?

A man's reproductive organs are the penis and testes (singular testis). The testes are contained in a skin sac called the scrotum. Running through the middle of the penis is a tube called the urethra. The urethra is connected to both the bladder and the testes. At different times, urine or sperm travel along the urethra and out of the man's body.

Where do sperm come from?

Sperm are made in the testes. They are manufactured in tiny tubes and are then stored in the epididymis, a long tube that is coiled on the surface of the testis. To pass to the woman's body, the sperm travel through two tubes called sperm ducts to the urethra inside the penis.

Why are the testes outside the body?

Sperm grow best at a temperature slightly below normal body temperature, so the testes hang outside the body to keep them cool.

How many sperm are made every day?

About 50 million sperm are made in each testis every day. They are either released, or destroyed and replaced with new sperm after a few days.

What does a sperm look like?

A sperm looks like a microscopic tadpole. The head of the sperm contains a nucleus, which fuses with the nucleus of the egg when fertilization occurs. In the middle section of the sperm are many mitochondria. These provide the sperm with energy to swim toward the egg. The sperm lashes its tail to push itself along.

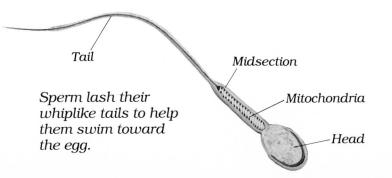

Tail

Midsection

Mitochondria

Sperm lash their whiplike tails to help them swim toward the egg.

Head

How fast do sperm swim?

Sperm can swim at up to 0.4 inch a minute. However, the journey to the egg takes them several hours.

An egg may be fertilized after sexual intercourse.

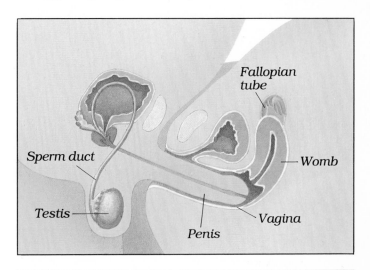

Fallopian tube

Sperm duct

Womb

Testis

Vagina

Penis

How far do sperm have to swim?

The distance from the cervix, through the womb, and up into the Fallopian tube is about 4 inches. Since sperm are only 0.002 inch long, this distance is roughly equivalent to someone swimming across the Atlantic!

How do sperm enter the woman's body?

Sperm enter the woman's body during sexual intercourse. The man's penis becomes stiff and is put inside the woman's vagina. Semen, a fluid containing the sperm, is squirted from the penis into the woman's vagina. This is called ejaculation. The fluid in semen contains nutrients and chemicals that stimulate the sperm to swim.

Why are so many sperm produced?

Sperm are produced in such great numbers to help ensure that one of them will fertilize the egg. An ejaculation contains 300 million sperm! However, many die before they reach the Fallopian tube. About half of the survivors then swim up the wrong tube. Only a few hundred sperm get close to the egg, and only one can fertilize it.

How does the egg leave the ovary?

A hollow, or follicle, forms on the surface of the ovary. This is where the egg ripens. The follicle bursts, releasing the egg into the Fallopian tube. The egg is then wafted along by tiny beating "hairs" lining the inside of the tube.

How do sperm find their way to the egg?

Chemical trails inside the cervix and womb lead the sperm into the Fallopian tubes. The egg itself also produces chemicals that attract the sperm directly to it.

Why do the sperm have to swim so far?

The sperm have to swim all the way up the Fallopian tube so that the egg is fertilized soon after its release. This gives the egg time to divide and grow while continuing its journey down the Fallopian tube to the womb.

What is the menstrual cycle?

Every month a ripe egg is released from the ovaries, and the lining of the womb develops so that it can receive a fertilized egg. If the egg is not fertilized the womb lining breaks down. This is called the menstrual cycle. It takes about 28 days and is controlled by hormones from the pituitary gland and the ovaries.

How does the womb prepare for pregnancy?

The womb's lining prepares for pregnancy by becoming thicker and rich in blood vessels. If fertilization does not take place, the lining is broken down. It is then shed through the vagina along with the unfertilized egg and some blood. This is called menstruation.

How often does menstruation occur?

Menstruation, or a period, occurs roughly every 28 days, at the start of each menstrual cycle. The bleeding usually lasts for four or five days. The womb lining then starts to develop once again.

What is contraception?

Contraception is another name for birth control. It refers to the variety of methods that prevent a woman from becoming pregnant. "Barrier" methods prevent the sperm from meeting the egg. Women can also take a contraceptive pill, which keeps the ovaries from making ripe eggs. There are many other birth control methods available to both women and men.

What happens if the egg is not fertilized?

If an egg is not fertilized after being released from the follicle, it will die within a few days.

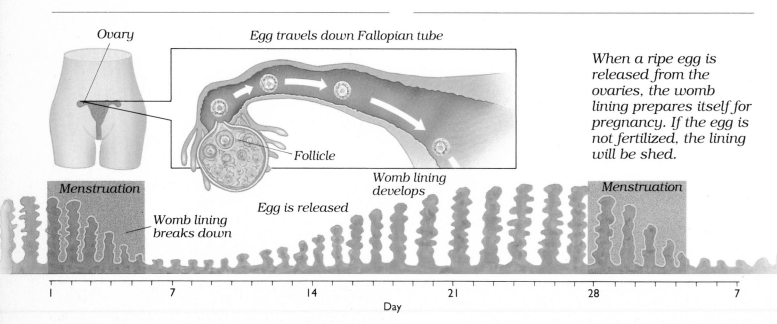

Ovary

Egg travels down Fallopian tube

Follicle

When a ripe egg is released from the ovaries, the womb lining prepares itself for pregnancy. If the egg is not fertilized, the lining will be shed.

Menstruation

Womb lining breaks down

Egg is released

Womb lining develops

Menstruation

Day

After Fertilization

What happens if the egg is fertilized?

If the egg is fertilized, its outer membrane swells into a jelly-like barrier to keep out other sperm. The fertilized egg travels down the Fallopian tube to the womb. As it does so it divides, first into two cells, then four, then eight. It arrives in the womb as a ball of about a hundred cells.

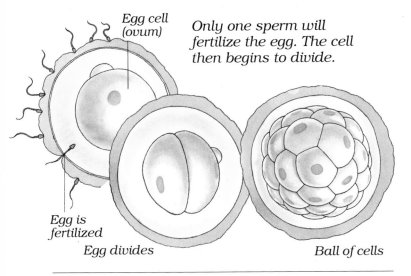

Egg cell (ovum)

Only one sperm will fertilize the egg. The cell then begins to divide.

Egg is fertilized

Egg divides

Ball of cells

What happens when the fertilized egg reaches the womb?

When the ball of cells arrives in the womb, it is still no bigger than a pinhead. It settles on the spongy lining of the womb. This is a process called implantation. Once the egg is firmly implanted, a woman is considered pregnant.

When does the ball of cells become an embryo?

The ball of cells is called an embryo for up to eight weeks after fertilization. The embryo forms from the ball of cells implanted in the mother's womb.

How is the embryo protected?

Some of the cells implanted in the womb develop into the amnion (a protective bag filled with fluid), which surrounds the embryo. The amnion acts as a shock absorber by keeping the embryo from being jolted.

What is the placenta?

The placenta is the embryo's life-support system. It forms after implantation from the most deeply embedded cells in the wall of the womb. It is a deep red disk-shaped organ containing many blood vessels. When it is fully developed it weighs about 1 pound. The placenta is the boundary between the embryo's blood circulation and the blood circulation of the mother. It is connected to the embryo by the umbilical cord.

What does the placenta do?

The embryo takes in food and oxygen from the mother's blood through the placenta. Waste products and carbon dioxide from the embryo pass back the other way. The placenta also acts as a barrier to keep germs and harmful substances from reaching the embryo.

What does the embryo look like?

In the first weeks of pregnancy it is difficult to tell a human embryo apart from those of other mammals. By the fourth week the embryo is about the size of a grain of rice. It has a recognizable head, a tail, and a body with segments that look a little like limbs. The brain, spinal cord, and gut have begun to form, and the developing heart has just begun beating.

At 7 weeks the embryo is about 1.2 inches long. Fingers and toes have begun to form.

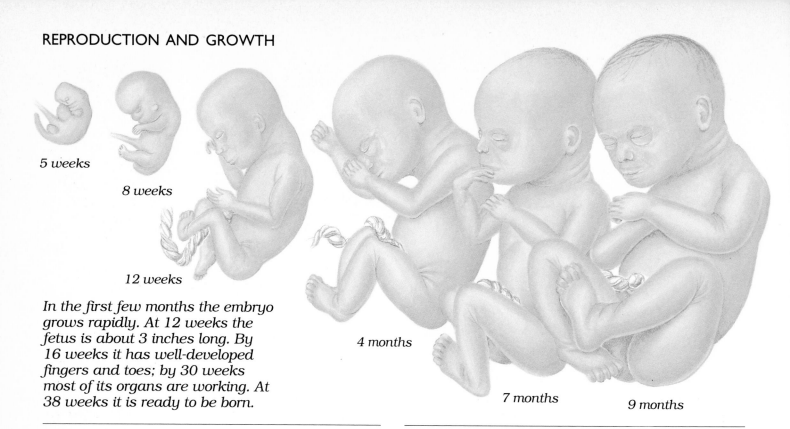

5 weeks

8 weeks

12 weeks

4 months

7 months

9 months

In the first few months the embryo grows rapidly. At 12 weeks the fetus is about 3 inches long. By 16 weeks it has well-developed fingers and toes; by 30 weeks most of its organs are working. At 38 weeks it is ready to be born.

How quickly does the embryo develop?

The embryo develops very quickly. Between the fourth and eighth week of pregnancy, the tail disappears. The embryo develops limbs, and its hands, feet, and facial features take shape. By eight weeks the embryo has a recognizable human form, and all of its major organ systems have started to develop.

What is a fetus?

When an embryo is eight weeks old, and its major organ systems have formed, it is called a fetus.

How quickly does the fetus develop?

The fetus grows very rapidly. By the 14th week, it is about 5 inches long. By then it has all of its internal organs, and its kidneys have just started to work.

When does the fetus start to kick?

By the 16th week, the mother begins to feel the fetus's first kicking movements. By the 20th week, the fetus has eyebrows, fingernails, and fingerprints. It is now about 7 inches long and weighs about 25 ounces.

What can harm a fetus?

Some germs, such as the virus that causes German measles, can travel across the placenta and harm the fetus. Alcohol in the mother's bloodstream, or the toxic products from smoking, may also pass through and harm the fetus.

What happens in the last 12 weeks before birth?

By 26 weeks the fetus has grown to about 10 inches long and weighs about 3.3 pounds. As the fetus grows larger there is less space for it to move. About two months before birth it comes to rest in a head-down position, ready to be born. Birth usually takes place around the 38th week of pregnancy.

How does the mother know when she is ready to give birth?

Labor pains are usually the first sign. These are contractions of the muscles of the womb, which the mother feels as cramps. The contractions become stronger, and the cervix, the opening of the womb, widens. The contractions force the baby's head down until the amnion breaks and the fluid inside is released through the vagina. Birth is not far off.

What happens when a baby is born?

Usually between six and twelve hours after the start of labor, the contractions of the womb muscles get much stronger. The mother pushes hard with her abdominal muscles, and the baby is gradually pushed out into the world through the cervix and vagina (birth canal).

What is the afterbirth?

The afterbirth is the placenta and the attached umbilical cord. Labor contractions force these out through the birth canal a few minutes after the baby is born.

What is a Cesarean section?

A Cesarean section is an operation that may be performed when a baby cannot be pushed out of the womb in the usual way. Doctors open the mother's abdomen and lift the baby out of the womb instead of allowing it to be born through the birth canal.

What is a premature baby?

A baby is premature if it is born too early and weighs less than 5.5 pounds. Premature babies often have difficulty breathing and feeding and are susceptible to infections. They are kept in an incubator until they reach a normal birth weight, but usually have regular contact with their mother during this time.

During childbirth, muscles in the womb squeeze to help push the baby out into the world.

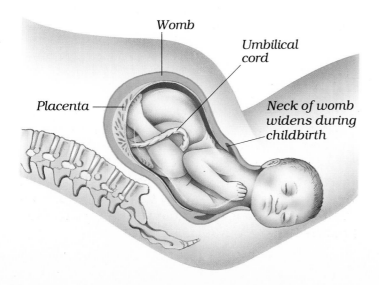

Womb

Umbilical cord

Placenta

Neck of womb widens during childbirth

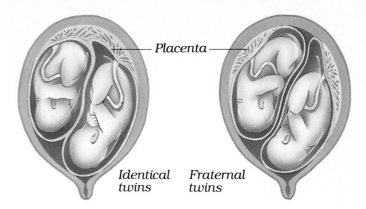

Placenta

Identical twins

Fraternal twins

Identical twins share a placenta in the womb; fraternal twins have separate placentas.

What are fraternal twins?

If two eggs are released by the mother's ovaries and both are fertilized, two fetuses develop with separate placentas. These are called fraternal twins. Although they share the womb, they are no more closely related than any other children with the same parents.

What are identical twins?

Sometimes the ball of cells formed after an egg is fertilized splits at an early stage and develops into two fetuses. Both fetuses share the same placenta. Because they come from the same egg and sperm, the two babies have exactly the same genes. They are called identical twins.

What is a multiple birth?

A multiple birth occurs when a pregnant woman gives birth to more than two children. The highest number of children ever produced from a multiple birth is ten.

Why are some people unable to have children?

There are several reasons why couples may be infertile (unable to have children). The man might not produce enough healthy sperm. The woman may not produce ripe eggs, or her Fallopian tubes might be blocked. Sometimes the cervix or womb does not provide a suitable environment for the sperm or eggs. Many of these conditions can be treated.

How can infertility be treated?

Fertility drugs that stimulate the ovaries to produce eggs may help infertile people. Another possible treatment is to fertilize the egg outside the woman's body.

What is a test-tube baby?

A test-tube baby does not grow inside a test tube. Eggs are taken from the woman and mixed, in a small glass dish, with sperm from the man. The eggs are fertilized and the young embryos are kept alive for a few days before they are placed in the woman's womb. The resulting babies are called test-tube babies.

When was the first test-tube baby born?

The world's first test-tube baby was born in England on July 25, 1978.

What are a newborn baby's reflexes?

When a baby's cheek is touched by the mother's breast, it automatically turns its head toward the breast. This "rooting reflex" helps the baby find the nipple for feeding. A baby will also grasp tightly any object placed in its palm. This is the grasp reflex. These instinctive actions are designed to protect the otherwise helpless baby.

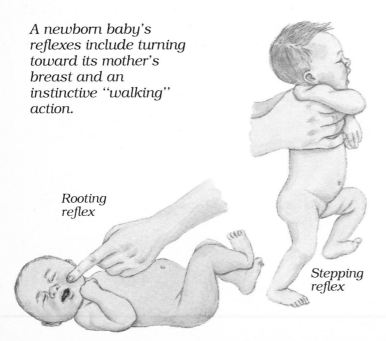

A newborn baby's reflexes include turning toward its mother's breast and an instinctive "walking" action.

Rooting reflex

Stepping reflex

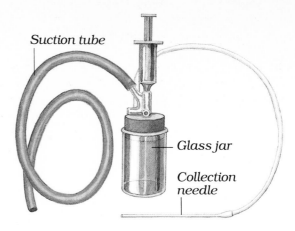

Suction tube

Glass jar

Collection needle

A test-tube baby develops from an egg that is fertilized outside the mother. A ripe egg is taken from the mother and fertilized in a glass dish.

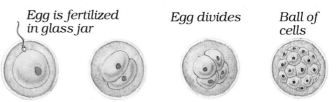

Egg is fertilized in glass jar

Egg divides

Ball of cells

After the fertilized egg has divided into 8 or 16 cells, it is implanted in the womb. The ball of cells then attaches itself to the womb lining.

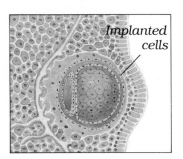

Womb lining

Ball of cells

Implanted cells

What can a newborn baby sense?

A newborn baby's sense of smell is much better than its sense of hearing or sight. It first learns to recognize its mother by smell.

Does a new baby have holes in its skull?

Not really. In order to fit its large head through the birth canal, a baby's skull bones must squeeze together and overlap. For this reason a newborn baby's bones contain a lot of cartilage and its skull bones are not fused together. The soft cartilage feels like a hole in the skull. During the first two years of life, the skeleton hardens and the skull bones fuse.

How do mothers produce milk?

During pregnancy, hormones cause the milk-producing glands (mammary glands) inside a mother's breast to develop. The glands start to release milk soon after she gives birth. When a baby feeds, the sucking action on the breast's nipple stimulates the release of milk.

What does the mother's milk contain?

The mother's milk contains exactly the right balance of carbohydrates, fats, proteins, vitamins, and minerals that the baby needs for growth during its first few months. After this, since the baby needs more iron and other nutrients, it needs to start eating other foods.

Is mother's milk better than powdered milk?

Powdered milk contains almost the same ingredients as human milk. But a mother's milk contains antibodies that help a baby fight disease. This gives mother's milk a slight advantage over prepared milk.

What happens in the first weeks of life?

In the first weeks of a baby's life many changes are taking place. For example, the blood that originally flowed through the umbilical vein and arteries when the baby was in the womb is rerouted through the lungs, liver, and heart. Also, a hole between the two sides of the heart seals up so the heart can function properly.

Why is a baby's head so big?

A baby needs a large brain to learn about its surroundings and respond to them. It therefore has a large head to house its brain. The brain makes up about 10 percent of a baby's body weight. (In an adult, the brain is only 2 percent of body weight.)

What can a baby do at three months?

At three months, a baby usually spends most of its time lying on its back. It can raise its head slightly, smile at its parents, and turn toward a noise. It can hold a rattle and will try to reach for toys, but its movements are jerky.

How developed is a baby at six months?

At six months a baby is twice its birth weight. It has strong neck and back muscles and can sit propped up. It is starting to make its first sounds. The baby uses its hands to scoop things up and put objects in its mouth. Its first teeth are coming through.

What is a baby like at twelve months?

A baby is now three times its weight at birth. It mostly crawls, but it can usually stand with support and walk a little while holding on to furniture. It is able to pick up objects carefully between its finger and thumb, and has learned to let go of objects. The baby can now recognize its name and may be able to say a few words.

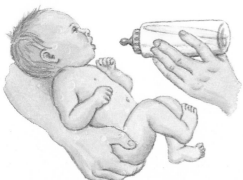

By three months a baby will lick his lips when he hears his food prepared.

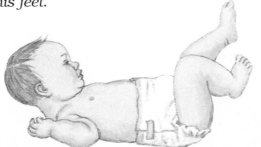

At six months a baby's neck muscles are getting stronger—he can lift his head to look at his feet.

A one-year-old can sit up for a long time and hold a cup with almost no help.

Growth and Development

Body proportions change in the womb and throughout our childhood.

(In womb)
3 months   6 months   Birth   18 months   6 years   12 years   18 years

Do we change shape as we grow?

Yes. At birth, our head is about one-quarter the length of our body. By age 18, our head is only one-eighth the length of our body. Our arms and legs get proportionally longer as we grow.

As a 3-month-old fetus, our head accounts for nearly half of our body size. We grow fastest inside the womb, and later around puberty (age 11 to 16 in girls, and 12 to 18 in boys).

How do we grow?

Most of our growth is due to an increase in the number of cells in our body. Cells divide and multiply, to form other cells. This process continues until we are fully grown.

What controls our growth?

Growth is controlled by a hormone produced by the pituitary gland. You actually grow a little faster at night, since this is when levels of the growth hormone are highest.

What is the average height for my age?

Since children grow at different rates, heights vary across an age group. The chart below gives average heights for boys and girls to age 18.

How quickly do children grow?

Children grow very quickly during the first two years of life. But from the age of three until around ten their growth becomes slow and steady. At puberty a new spurt of growth takes place. This spurt ends around the age of 18.

What is adolescence?

Adolescence is the time between when you are a child and when you become an adult. It is a period of rapid growth and physical and emotional change. Adolescence starts with puberty.

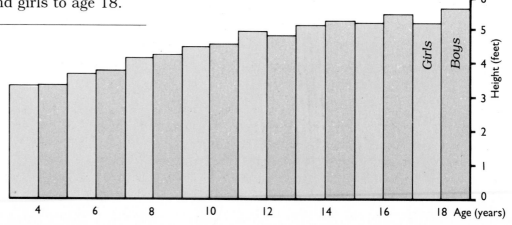

A comparison of heights up to age 18 shows that, generally, girls are taller than boys only around the age of 12, when girls start their growth spurt.

Girls   Boys

Height (feet)

4   6   8   10   12   14   16   18 Age (years)

What is puberty?

Puberty is the period in our life when the sex organs mature and other physical changes occur. During puberty, girls and boys begin to develop into men and women.

What happens to a boy during puberty?

During puberty, a boy's penis and testes get larger, and he starts producing sperm. His build changes, and his torso gets larger. He can grow a beard and his body hair becomes thicker, particularly under the arms and in the groin area. His voicebox (larynx) develops and his voice gets deeper.

Why do boys' voices change?

The bigger the larynx, and the longer the vocal cords, the deeper the voice. At puberty boys' vocal cords grow much more rapidly than girls', so their voices suddenly become deeper.

What happens to a girl during puberty?

During puberty, a girl's ovaries mature and her menstrual cycle begins. Her breasts develop and her hips widen. Body hair develops under the arms and in the groin area.

What triggers the changes of puberty?

In both boys and girls, puberty is triggered by the pituitary gland in the brain. The pituitary stimulates other glands to release sex hormones. In boys, the changes are triggered by testosterone, which is produced by the testes. In girls they are triggered by estrogen, which is produced by the ovaries.

Why are some teenagers argumentative?

The teenage years can be a difficult time. Young people are adjusting both to a changing body and a new role in life. They may soon be going out to work or leaving home to study. They are becoming more independent and are starting to think for themselves. Because they feel like adults but may still be treated like children, teenagers may come in conflict with adults.

Your teenage years are a time for making new friends, learning more about the world around you, and preparing for adulthood.

When do we become adults?

Biologically, we become adults when we have reached sexual maturity and have stopped growing. In girls this is likely to be by the late teens and in boys by the early twenties.

When are we at our physical peak?

We are at our physical peak in our twenties. This is when we have stopped growing and are at our strongest physically. Our body has yet to decline through wear and tear.

What is menopause?

In middle age, a woman's periods become less regular and eventually stop altogether. This is because her ovaries are no longer producing ripe eggs. This change marks the end of the time in which she can have children. It is known as menopause.

How does my body know when to stop growing?

Nobody knows for sure. It seems that our cells have a built-in stopwatch. After dividing a certain number of times, they stop dividing. For example, connective tissue cells grown in a laboratory stopped dividing after about 50 cell divisions. (Nerve cells are an exception—they never divide after forming.)

What is aging?

Aging is a natural process that occurs when some of the body's cells gradually become less efficient and eventually die. This process happens to everybody, but the rate at which it takes place varies from person to person.

What causes aging?

Many of the changes during aging are part of a built-in plan: they are determined by your genes. Other changes are the result of your lifestyle or the effects of your environment. Stiff joints, for example, could result from lack of exercise; dry skin could be due to too much sun.

Does long life run in the family?

Yes. Aside from accidental death, how long you live seems to be inherited to some extent. It seems that some families are less prone to disease and the effects of aging.

What happens to our senses as we grow old?

Sight, hearing, smell, and taste all deteriorate as we grow old. Since the lens of our eye becomes less flexible, close-focusing becomes difficult and we may need reading glasses. Also, our hearing loses its edge. In particular, we cannot hear high-pitched sounds well, and may start to miss high notes in pieces of music.

Why do some people get ill more often when they get old?

As we grow old our body's defenses become less effective in combating disease. Our antibodies may even start attacking our own body. Rheumatoid arthritis—a painful inflammation of the joints—can be caused by a person's antibodies attacking the membranes in their joints.

Can we slow the aging process?

Yes, we can, by remaining both physically and mentally active. Physical activity helps blood circulation, while mental activity keeps the brain alert.

What changes take place inside our bodies as we get older?

As we get older the heart and arteries shrink slightly and their walls become less elastic. Hardening of the arteries, thrombosis (a stroke), and hemorrhages (bleeding) are more likely. The lungs are not as efficient at picking up oxygen, partly because of the reduced blood supply and partly because the lung tissues themselves are affected. These changes in the lungs and circulation affect all organs by reducing their oxygen supply.

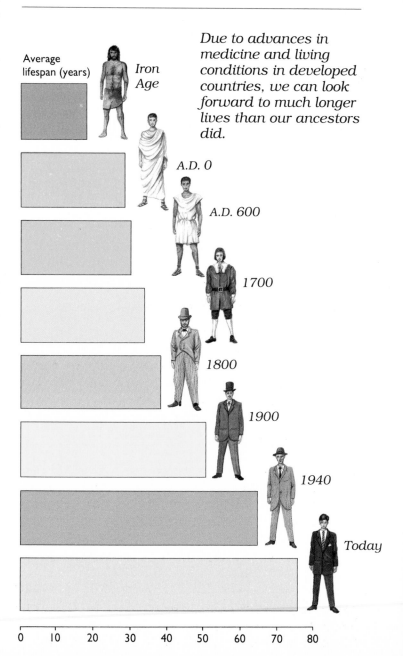

Average lifespan (years)

Iron Age

A.D. 0

A.D. 600

1700

1800

1900

1940

Today

Due to advances in medicine and living conditions in developed countries, we can look forward to much longer lives than our ancestors did.

0 10 20 30 40 50 60 70 80

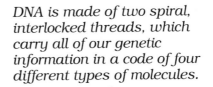

Genetics

What is genetics?

Genetics is the study of heredity—the passing of characteristics from parent to child.

What are chromosomes?

Chromosomes are microscopic, threadlike structures found in the nucleus of every cell (although they become visible only when the cell is dividing). Chromosomes contain all the necessary information for the cell to develop.

How many chromosomes are there in a cell?

Human cells normally contain 46 chromosomes, which come in 22 matching pairs, plus a special pair that determines the sex of the individual.

What is a gene?

A gene is a short section of a chromosome. The gene carries a set of instructions that determines one of the individual's characteristics, such as eye color.

How many genes do we have?

It is difficult to say exactly, but we have at least 10,000 types of genes. Each carries instructions for making a protein. Proteins make up major parts of every cell. They determine the way the cells work, which, in turn, gives us our features.

What is DNA?

DNA (short for deoxyribonucleic acid) is the complicated chemical substance that makes up our genes and chromosomes. DNA contains the genetic information that is passed from one generation to the next.

About half our genes have come from each parent, which is why we may look so like them. Actor Charlie Sheen looks much like his father, Martin.

DNA is made of two spiral, interlocked threads, which carry all of our genetic information in a code of four different types of molecules.

What is the double helix?

The DNA molecule is made of two long interlocked strands that coil around each other, like a twisted rope ladder. This structure is known as the double helix.

Why are we a mixture of our parents?

The male sperm cells and female egg cells contain only 23 chromosomes each—half the number found in any other cell. When the nuclei of these two cells come together in a fertilized egg, the chromosomes combine to make 46 chromosomes in all. All the cells in our body originally came from a fertilized egg, so half the genetic information in every cell has come from our father, and half from our mother. This means that we will grow up with a mixture of features from both parents.

When is a gene "dominant"?

Most of our characteristics are controlled by two genes—one gene from each parent. These genes can be identical, but often they are not. For example, you may have genes for two different eye colors. If you have a gene for brown eyes from one parent and a gene for blue eyes from the other, the brown-eye gene will override the blue-eye one. You will have brown eyes. The gene for brown eyes is said to be "dominant" and the one for blue eye color, "recessive."

Which features do we inherit from our parents?

We inherit features such as skin color, hair color, and overall body shape. Our features may be a combination of both parents, or we may look much more like one than the other. We also inherit permanent features such as our blood type.

Which characteristics do we not inherit?

Some of our features are influenced by the way we live our lives, rather than the genes that we inherit. For example, our fitness depends on our lifestyle. Characteristics that develop as the result of an accident, such as a scar from a bad cut, are not inherited or passed on to our children.

How can you inherit a feature that your parents do not have?

This can happen if both your parents carry the same recessive gene. For example, if both parents are brown-eyed but each also carries the recessive gene for blue eyes, there is a one-in-four chance that their child will be blue-eyed.

What are X and Y chromosomes?

The X and Y chromosomes make up the 23rd pair of chromosomes. They determine the sex of an individual. A woman has two X chromosomes, while a man has one X and one Y. The X chromosome is longer than the Y chromosome, and so part of it is unmatched.

Are there such things as "bad" genes?

Yes. Some genes do not seem to do us any good at all. Hemophilia—the condition where blood fails to clot normally—is one example. Hemophilia is caused by a defective gene on the X chromosome.

How is hemophilia inherited?

The gene for hemophilia is carried on the X chromosome and is overridden by (or recessive to) the normal gene. Because women have two X chromosomes, the hemophilia gene would need to be present on both chromosomes for a woman to suffer from the condition. However, if the gene is present on one of her X chromosomes, the woman is a carrier, and her sons may be hemophiliacs. A man has only one X chromosome, so if he has the hemophilia gene, he will have the condition. As a result, hemophilia is much more common in men than in women. If a male hemophiliac has children with a noncarrier, his children will not have the disease.

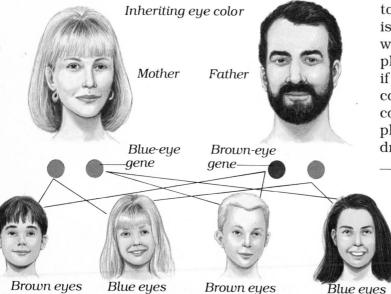

Inheriting eye color

Mother   *Father*

Blue-eye gene   *Brown-eye gene*

Brown eyes   *Blue eyes*   *Brown eyes*   *Blue eyes*

One gene from each parent decides eye color. In this family, the father has a blue-eye and a brown-eye gene, whereas the mother has two blue-eye genes. The chart shows the possible combinations of genes in their children.

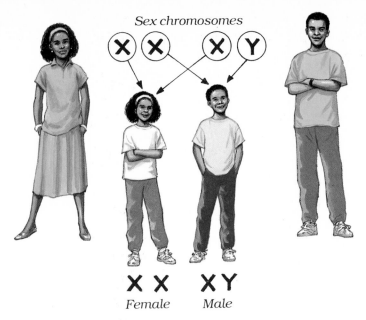

A baby's sex depends on whether the father's sperm carries an X chromosome (for a girl) or a Y chromosome (for a boy).

When is a baby's sex decided?

A baby's sex is decided at the moment of fertilization, by the sex chromosome in the father's sperm. All the mother's eggs carry an X chromosome, while about half the father's sperm carry an X and half carry a Y. If a Y-carrying sperm fertilizes the egg, the baby will be XY—a boy. If an X-carrying sperm fertilizes the egg, the baby will be XX—a girl.

Why are more men color-blind than women?

Color blindness is linked to an individual's sex. The recessive gene for red-green color blindness is carried on the X chromosome. If a man has this gene, he will be color-blind, but a woman would need two copies of this gene (one on each X chromosome) to be color-blind.

How often are people color-blind?

About 1 man in 12 is partially red-green color-blind, but only 1 woman in 250 is affected.

What can we find out from family trees?

Family trees are diagrams that show us how traits are inherited. Hemophilia can be traced through female carriers, for example.

What is a mutation?

A mutation is a sudden change in the genetic material (the DNA) inside a cell. Mutations affect genes and chromosomes and alter the instructions contained in them. The most serious mutations are those that take place in the cells that produce eggs and sperm, since these mutations can be passed on to offspring.

What is a gene mutation?

A gene mutation is a small change in the DNA that affects only one gene. For example, the gene for hemophilia is such a mutation.

What is a chromosome mutation?

A chromosome mutation is a major change in the DNA of the cell that affects a large part or all of a chromosome.

What is Down's syndrome?

Down's syndrome is a condition caused by the presence of an extra chromosome in the body's cells. A Down's syndrome child has 47 chromosomes instead of 46. This results in characteristic broad faces and reduced mental ability.

Down's syndrome is caused by the presence of an extra chromosome in the cells.

THE BRAIN

What does the brain look like?

From above, the brain looks rather like a giant walnut, pink-gray and wrinkled. It has the consistency of thick pudding.

What is the brain made of?

The brain is a mass of over 10 billion nerve cells. These are surrounded and supported by cells called glia, which supply them with nutrients.

What does the brain do?

The brain is the body's control center. It sends and receives messages to and from organs and tissues all over the body. The brain gives us our ability to learn, reason, and feel. It controls our voluntary, or conscious, activities, as well as involuntary activities we are not aware of.

Different regions of the brain process different types of information.

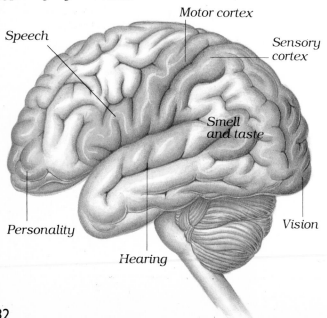

Speech

Motor cortex

Sensory cortex

Smell and taste

Personality

Hearing

Vision

How is the brain protected?

The skull protects the brain from most physical injuries. The brain is also protected by three layers of tissue, called meninges, which are wrapped around it. The inner layer acts as a barrier to prevent bacteria from reaching the brain. The middle layer contains cerebrospinal fluid. This supplies the brain with food and oxygen and acts as a shock absorber, cushioning the brain against damage. The outer layer lines the cranium, or skull.

How heavy is the brain?

On average, an adult male brain weighs about 3 pounds. At birth a baby's brain weighs less than a pound. By the time the child is about five years old, the brain has reached 90 percent of its full adult weight.

How complicated is the human brain?

The human brain is the world's most complex living structure. Each of its 10 billion nerve cells is connected to as many as 10,000 other nerve cells. This means that there are billions of different connections and pathways that messages can take through the brain.

How is the brain like a computer?

Like a computer, the brain is made up of circuits that carry electrical signals. The brain's circuits are made up of nerve cells instead of transistors. As in a computer, some of the circuits in the brain form a memory to store information, and others are used to process incoming information and respond to it.

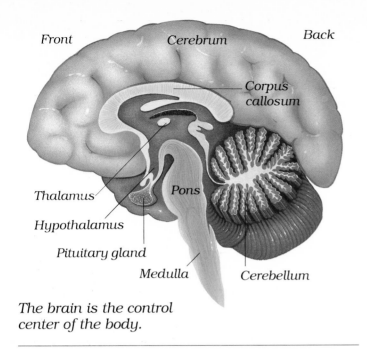

Front Cerebrum Back

Corpus callosum

Thalamus Pons

Hypothalamus

Pituitary gland

Medulla Cerebellum

The brain is the control center of the body.

What are the main parts of the brain?

The three main parts of the brain are the cerebrum (at the top), the medulla (on the underside), and the cerebellum (at the back). The cerebrum is divided into two halves called hemispheres.

Which is the largest part of the brain?

By far, the largest part of the brain is the cerebrum, which makes up about 85 percent of the brain's weight. It is the cerebrum that gives us our intelligence and our emotions. We use it to think, feel, and remember.

Why does the brain look wrinkled?

The outer edge of the cerebrum, where most of our thinking goes on, is called the cerebral cortex. It is only 0.1 inch thick but is about the size of a page from a tabloid newspaper. Since it has to be scrunched together and packed tightly into the skull, the brain looks very wrinkled.

What is the brain stem?

The brain stem is the long area that connects the brain and spinal cord. It is thought to be the first part of the brain to have evolved. The medulla and hypothalamus (see p. 84) are located in the brain stem.

What does the medulla do?

Most of our involuntary activities (those that work automatically) are controlled by the medulla, at the base of the brain. Breathing and heartbeat are some of the activities controlled by the medulla.

What does the cerebellum do?

The cerebellum coordinates the body's movements so that our actions are smooth and well controlled. It receives messages from receptors in our muscles and joints and from the organs of balance in our inner ear.

What is gray matter?

Gray matter is the part of the brain and spinal cord that contains the nerve cell bodies. The nuclei in the cell bodies make the tissue look gray. Most gray matter in the brain is found in the outer part (the cerebral cortex). In the spinal cord the gray matter is on the inside.

Where is white matter found?

Most of the inner part of the brain is made up of white matter. White matter is also found in the spinal cord. It is the part of the brain and spinal cord that contains mostly nerve fibers.

Gray matter, found in the cerebral cortex and spinal cord, consists of nerve cell bodies and dendrites. White matter contains the long, insulated nerve fibers.

Brain

Gray matter

Spinal cord

White matter

How are the two halves of the brain joined together?

The right and left cerebral hemispheres are joined together by bundles of nerve fibers. The largest bundle is called the corpus callosum.

Why is it important to keep the brain well supplied with oxygen?

Even though the brain makes up only 2 percent of the body's weight, it uses up 20 percent of the body's energy. Because of this, the brain must have a constant supply of blood, bringing food and oxygen to keep it working properly. If the brain does not get enough blood you may feel faint. Brain cells start to die after about three minutes without oxygen.

Can brain damage be repaired?

Once brain cells are destroyed they can never be replaced. However, other brain cells can sometimes take over the job of the damaged cells.

What is the hypothalamus?

The hypothalamus is a small region in the center of the brain. It is incredibly important for controlling some of the body's automatic functions. Not only does it control our body temperature, heartbeat, and kidney function, but it helps control our hunger and thirst and our sleeping patterns as well.

Is the left side of your brain connected to the left side of your body?

No. The left side of the brain is connected to the right side of the body. The nerve cells that carry messages from the brain cross over at the base of the brain. Signals from the left go to the right side of the body, and vice versa.

Why are most people right-handed?

In most people, the left side of the brain is dominant over the right side. Since the left cortex controls movements in the right side of the body, most people have better control with their right hand.

Do the right and left halves of the brain do different jobs?

Yes. In most people the left side controls speaking, writing, and logical thinking. The right side is more artistic and creative. Most of us seem to use one side more than the other.

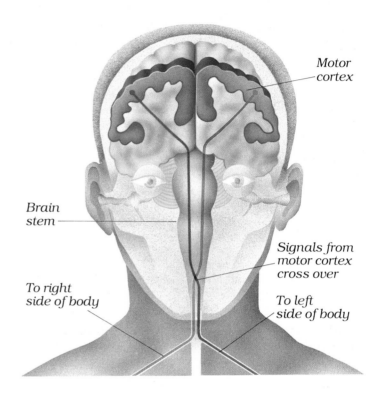

As signals from each side of the cortex pass through the brain stem they cross over and travel to the opposite side of the body.

Are men's brains bigger than women's?

On average, women's brains are a little smaller than men's. However, women have smaller bodies than men—and so, pound for pound, women's brains are at least the size of men's.

How quickly does our brain develop?

At birth, the brain already has most of its nerve cells and makes up 10 percent of body weight. After birth, the nerve cells increase in size and develop many connections between them (this is known as the "wiring" of the brain). It is in the first few years of life that much of the brain's development takes place.

Does our brain shrink as we get older?

As children our brains keep growing, reaching their maximum size and weight in our early twenties. After this, brain cells start to die off, a few at a time. Luckily, we have so many brain cells that this does not usually cause a problem.

What happens when the brain receives a signal?

When signals are sent from sense organs to the brain, they are directed to a special part of the cerebral cortex called the sensory area. This interprets the message and "informs" the rest of the cortex about it. If the cortex "decides" to respond in some way, messages are sent from a specialized region called the motor area to muscles or glands to produce the response.

Are girls' brains different from boys'?

Maybe. As a rule, most boys are better at tasks that require "spatial ability"—picturing the shape and position of objects or patterns. Girls are better at using words, and usually learn to read at an earlier age. However, this also could be caused by the different ways boys and girls are brought up.

Picturing your next move in a chess game involves the visual skills of the right side of your brain. As you talk to yourself about what your opponent might then do, you are using the verbal skills of the left side.

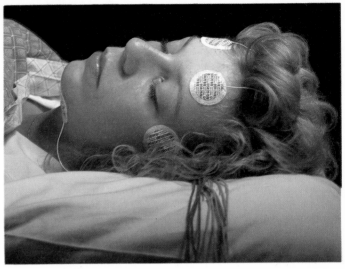

The brain's electrical activity can be measured by attaching electrodes to someone's scalp. The changes in activity are analyzed by computer.

What are brain waves?

These are waves of electrical activity produced by the nerve cells of the cerebrum. Brain waves can be picked up by a machine called an electro-encephalograph. Electrodes attached to the scalp record a person's brain waves. These are traced onto a screen or paper. The recording of the brain waves is called an electro-encephalogram (EEG).

Does the brain feel pain?

The feeling of pain is created by the brain in another part of the body. However, the brain itself has no pain receptors. When the brain is operated on, no pain is felt. Occasionally, brain surgery can be carried out under local anesthetic, while the patient is awake.

Why is the brain "mapped"?

Scientists "map" the brain to try to figure out the functions of its different parts. This is done in two ways. One is to study people who have had part of their brain accidentally damaged and record what effect this has had on them. Another way of mapping the brain is to pass a weak electrical current through parts of it, using electrodes, and then to ask the person what they are experiencing. This is done with the person's permission and is not painful!

Memory and Learning

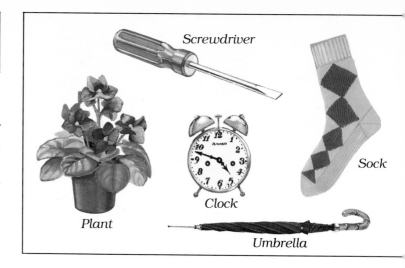

Screwdriver

Sock

Clock

Plant

Umbrella

What is the mind?

The mind is the part of us that gives rise to our thoughts, memories, and feelings. It is believed that the mind is situated in the brain.

What is the subconscious?

The subconscious is the part of the mind that we are not aware of. It can affect the way we behave, but we do not normally realize it.

What is memory?

Memory is our ability to store the things we learn and experience in our lives. Memory involves three stages: the mind receives information, stores it, and later retrieves it.

Are there different types of memory?

There are three types of memory. Sensory memory is the memory of the world around us at any one moment. It allows us to find our way about without bumping into things. Short-term memory lasts for about 30 seconds. For example, it allows you to remember a telephone number while you search for paper to write it down. Long-term memory may last for years.

We use a different memory store for these activities: (a) long-term, (b) short-term, (c) sensory memory.

How many things can we remember?

We can remember a list of about seven things at the same time. This is why most people have difficulty in remembering a telephone number with more than seven figures. But if the numbers are grouped, it makes them easier to remember, because your memory can hold about seven "bundles" or groups of information.

Where do we keep our memories?

We keep our memories in our brain, but not all in one place. It seems that particular memories are stored in several places in the cerebral cortex. Even if one part of the brain is damaged, the memories it held are not always lost.

How do I store something in my long-term memory?

Something that "leaves a mark on your mind," or is especially interesting, is likely to stay in your long-term memory. Repeating information when you study for a test will help you remember it.

What is amnesia?

Amnesia is the sudden loss of memory. It is very rare. It may occur when a person has had a bad shock, but there is often no apparent cause of amnesia. The loss of memory is usually selective (only some things are forgotten), and most everyday activities are remembered. The memory of someone with amnesia usually comes back within a few hours, days, or weeks.

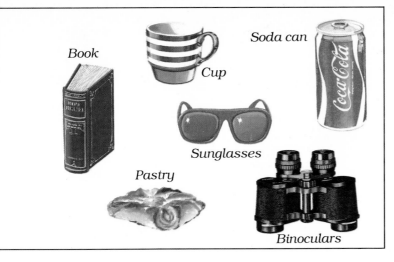

Book

Cup

Soda can

Sunglasses

Pastry

Binoculars

Test your memory. Look at the objects above for about 30 seconds, then cover them up. How many can you remember?

How do we learn?

We learn in many different ways. When we learn facts for a classroom test, we may soon forget them. When we learn a skill like riding a bicycle or swimming, it may stay with us for a lifetime. Without a doubt, much of our early learning comes from copying our elders.

What is a photographic memory?

A few people have the ability to memorize a picture, page, or scene as though it were a photograph in their mind's eye. They can recall the precise location of objects in a picture or specific words in a particular place on a page. Most of us create pictures in our mind to recall past events, but very few people have the ability to recall information with the detail and accuracy of a photograph.

What is insight learning?

Insight learning is a form of reasoning in which we use past experience to find a solution to a new problem. It is found in humans and other intelligent animals such as chimpanzees. For example, if a chimpanzee is left in a room with a bunch of bananas hanging from the ceiling and some boxes, it will use insight to reach the fruit. After some thinking, the chimp will make a pile of the boxes and climb up to the bananas.

What is instinct?

An instinctive action is something we can do without having to learn it. A newborn baby will automatically suck its mother's breast. This instinctive behavior helps the baby survive, since it needs to be able to feed right away and cannot afford to spend time learning how.

What did Pavlov's dogs do?

Ivan Pavlov was a Russian biologist who studied a type of learning called classical conditioning in dogs. For several days, Pavlov rang a bell when he fed the dogs. Later, the sound of the bell alone caused the dogs' mouths to water. They were conditioned to associate the bell with food, and so responded to it in the same way.

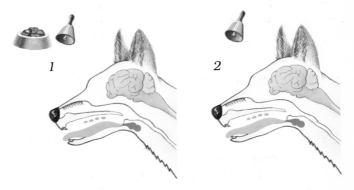

1

2

In Pavlov's experiment to show conditioning, a bell was rung every time the dogs were fed (1). After a while the dogs' mouths would water at the sound of the bell even if there was no food (2).

What are conditioned reflexes?

Conditioned reflexes are movements that we coordinate consciously at first, but learn to perform automatically. Learning to play tennis or to type develops many conditioned reflexes.

What did Skinner's rats do?

The American scientist B. F. Skinner worked with caged rats to show a type of conditioning. A starved rat discovered that when it pressed a lever, food was immediately delivered. The rat came to associate pressing the lever with the arrival of food, and so was encouraged to operate the lever more often to get more food.

Personality and Intelligence

What is intelligence?

Psychologists (scientists who study the mind) cannot agree on an exact definition of intelligence. Put simply, intelligence is mental ability—the ability to reason, learn, and understand. There are many different ways to show intelligence, from writing an original story to solving a problem in math. Intelligence covers many different mental skills, and most people are better at some skills than others.

Detecting patterns is one kind of intelligence. In each set below, the left-hand pictures follow a pattern. Choose one picture from the right-hand column to complete each set. (Answers on p. 89)

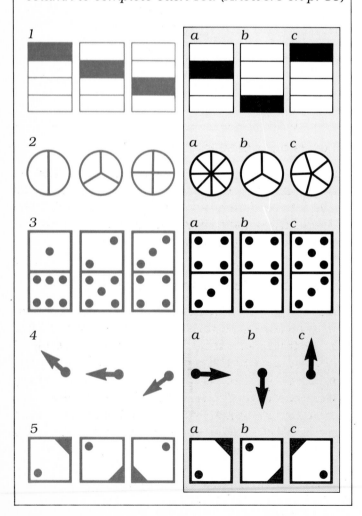

What is IQ?

IQ, or intelligence quotient, is one measure of a person's intelligence. It is calculated by taking a written IQ test. Usually this involves choosing the correct answer from a choice of several possible answers. The average IQ score is 100.

Is IQ a good measure of intelligence?

IQ may be a rough measure of intelligence but it has a number of drawbacks. There are several different types of intelligence and an IQ test does not measure all of them. For example, some people are extremely good at music or art, but this is not measured by an IQ test. Also, some people are better at IQ tests than others, because they have practiced doing them. Some people feel that the IQ test is geared toward certain groups of people, as these groups seem to do better on them.

Why are humans so intelligent?

Humans are more intelligent than other animals because we have a much larger cerebrum. This gives us a greater ability to reason and allows us to communicate our ideas using language. In this way, knowledge is spread rapidly and can be passed from one generation to the next. Our ability to stand on two legs frees our hands for tool making, which also enables us to do far more than other animals.

Is intelligence inherited?

Intelligence is inherited to some degree, but the environment you are brought up in—for example how you are encouraged to play, read, and work—plays a very important part as well. A good environment helps you to make the most of the abilities you have inherited.

Are people with the biggest brains the most intelligent?

No. Your intelligence does not closely tie in with the size of your brain. Geniuses do not have larger brains than other people. The biggest brain ever recorded weighed about 4.5 pounds, but its owner was not exceptionally intelligent.

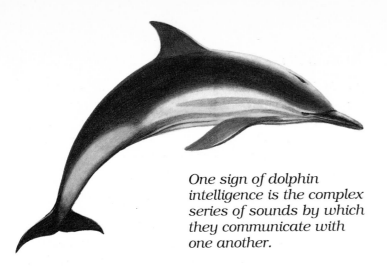

One sign of dolphin intelligence is the complex series of sounds by which they communicate with one another.

What is the most intelligent animal?

After humans, the most intelligent animals may be either chimpanzees or dolphins. Both of these animals have good problem-solving and communication skills.

What are the silent areas of the brain?

Certain areas of the brain are called "silent" because they do not produce a sensation or response when they are electrically stimulated. They seem to be responsible for character and personality. They are found at the front of the cerebral cortex.

What is personality?

Personality describes an individual's particular characteristics, such as whether they are loud or quiet, serious, or happy-go-lucky. Personality is sometimes measured in terms of whether a person is an extrovert or introvert. Most of us are neither completely one type nor the other.

What is an extrovert?

An extrovert is someone who tends to be outgoing and likes mixing with people. Extroverts like change and are inclined to act on impulse.

What is an introvert?

An introvert is the opposite of an extrovert. Introverts tend to be quiet, retiring, and reliable. They think deeply about things and have a small circle of friends.

What is the inkblot test?

The inkblot test involves looking at several inkblot shapes and interpreting what the images are or mean. It is used as a way of testing people's personalities and understanding their unconscious feelings and wishes.

The images people see in the inkblot test may provide a clue to their unconscious wishes or reflect their state of mind.

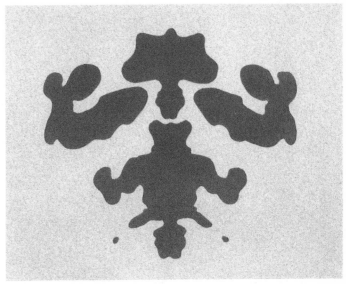

When is our personality formed?

Our personality is a blend of the qualities we inherit and the way we respond to influences in our lives, such as family and friends. An individual's personality begins to emerge in the first weeks and months of their life.

Where do our feelings come from?

When we go about our everyday lives we respond to the pictures, sounds, and smells around us. Our feelings, or emotions, are another type of response to what we experience. Feelings are produced in the brain. They involve many areas, particularly the hypothalamus and the cerebrum. Feelings arise as a result of nerve signals coming from a sensory organ, or from the cortex, in response to our thoughts.

*Answers to intelligence test on page 88:
1 (b), 2 (c), 3 (a), 4 (b), 5 (c)*

Communication

What is communication?

Communication is the passing of a message from one person to another. Communication using language is verbal communication. All other forms of communication, from our tone of voice to body movements, are nonverbal.

How do babies communicate?

Babies begin to communicate by crying. A mother or father can soon distinguish different types of crying. The cry a baby makes when it is hungry is different from that when it is tired or frustrated. Facial expressions are important too. Within a few months of birth, babies communicate their moods by smiling or frowning.

How quickly do we learn language?

As babies, we start to babble. We are learning to make the sounds used in language. Babies can make all of the sounds used in every language in the world. But they learn to select and use those they hear most often. By the age of about one year or so we say our first words. By two years we have a vocabulary of several hundred words and can speak in short phrases. By three we speak in sentences, and by four we have learned the basic rules of grammar.

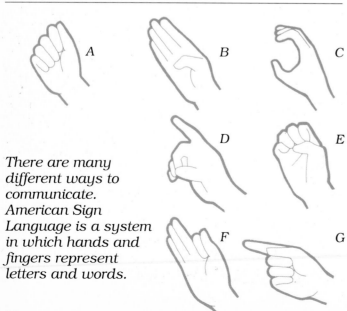

There are many different ways to communicate. American Sign Language is a system in which hands and fingers represent letters and words.

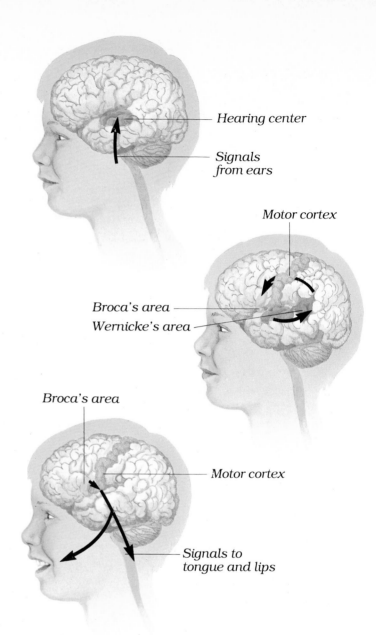

Hearing center

Signals from ears

Motor cortex

Broca's area

Wernicke's area

Broca's area

Motor cortex

Signals to tongue and lips

In the brain, sound is interpreted by Wernicke's area, and the cortex prepares a reply. Broca's area supplies the instructions for the muscle movements required for speaking a word. The motor cortex organizes the movements.

Which areas of the brain control speech?

Two areas of the left cerebral hemisphere control speech. Broca's area is responsible for forming speech, while a separate region, Wernicke's area, is responsible for making sense of speech. Both regions were identified in the nineteenth century by scientists who examined the effects of accidental brain damage on patients' speech. The two areas are now named after these scientists.

How many languages are there?

There are about 5,000 different languages in the world. The most common language is Mandarin Chinese, which is spoken by an estimated 600 million people. English is next. It is spoken by nearly 400 million people.

How large is your vocabulary?

There are about 600,000 words in the English language. On average, a person uses less than 10,000 of these, or less than 2 percent of the words available. Someone can be fluent in English knowing only 2,000 words.

Who spoke the most languages?

Dr. Harold Williams of New Zealand (1876–1928) spoke 58 languages. When he attended the League of Nations conference in Geneva, Switzerland, he was the only person who could speak to every delegate in his own language.

What is dyslexia?

People with dyslexia, or "word blindness," have difficulty reading and spelling. Some common mistakes include reversing letters (such as "b" and "d") or words ("was" and "saw"). Dyslexia can be helped to some extent by special teaching and learning methods.

What causes a stutter?

We are not exactly sure what causes a stutter. It may be that the brain cannot check properly what has just been said. Or it could be caused by poor coordination of the palate, tongue, and lips. About four out of every hundred people stutter, though some only slightly. Special speech therapy helps many people get over or improve their stuttering.

What is body language?

Body language is nonverbal communication or any communication other than what we say. This includes the pitch of our voice, our facial expression, our gestures and hand movements, and how we stand.

What do people's hand gestures tell us?

Hand gestures such as the thumbs-up sign may be used consciously. However, we often use gestures unconsciously, and these can betray secrets we are trying to hide. A child telling a lie will often conceal her mouth with her hands.

Are hand gestures the same the world over?

No. Hand gestures can mean different things in different cultures. The thumbs-up sign means "OK" in English-speaking countries. In France it also means "zero," and in Japan it means "money." In some countries it is a rude gesture.

What is social behavior?

Social behavior is the way we act when we are with other people. In particular, it is the behavior of someone in a group such as a family, a group of friends, or a class at school.

What is peer pressure?

Peer pressure is the pressure a group of people puts on an individual to behave in a particular way. For example, in a group of friends you may feel under pressure to like the same music and clothes as the others.

As we speak, our facial expressions and hand gestures add emphasis to what we say.

Sleep and Dreaming

Why do we need to sleep?

No one is exactly sure why we need to sleep. Of course, sleeping rests the body, but it is also thought that during sleep we repair our tissues, grow new cells, and recover from the day's activities. Our brains are still very active while we sleep. Some people think that the brain sorts through the day's events during this time, organizing new information and fitting it in with previous information. This may help us to learn from new experiences.

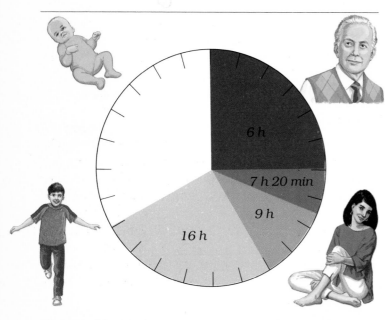

We need less sleep as we grow older. A baby must sleep for 16 hours a day; a 12-year-old, for 9 hours; a young adult, for 7 hours and 20 minutes; and a 65-year-old, for 6 hours.

How much sleep do we need?

On average, we sleep about 8 hours a day; spread over a lifetime, that makes more than 20 years! The amount of sleep we need varies greatly from one person to another, but it seems we need less sleep as we get older. A newborn baby needs 16 hours of sleep each day; a 65-year-old needs only 6 hours. As a general rule, we sleep more when we are recovering from an illness or injury.

What happens when we sleep?

As we go to sleep our heart rate falls, our blood pressure drops, and our breathing becomes slow and regular. After about 20 minutes, our body usually stops shifting around and we settle into a deep sleep called orthodox sleep. Our muscles are relaxed and our brain activity is slowed. It is during orthodox sleep that most of the growth, maintenance, and repair of our body occurs. This sleep is broken up by periods of shallow sleep and REM (rapid eye movement) sleep.

How did REM sleep get its name?

REM sleep got its name from the rapid back-and-forth movement of our eyes under our eyelids. It is during this sleep that most of our dreaming occurs.

What is sleepwalking?

Sleepwalking (somnambulism) affects children more often than adults. Nobody quite knows what causes sleepwalking. It occurs during orthodox sleep, and the parts of the brain that control movement and speech stay awake. The person may speak, sit up, and even walk around. Their senses are partly awake, but they do not remember anything when they wake up.

Sleep gives the body time to rest and repair itself and get ready for the day ahead.

What are the different stages of sleep?

If we sleep 8 hours in one night, perhaps 3 to 4 hours is orthodox sleep, mixed up with 2 to 3 hours of REM sleep and 1 to 2 hours of shallow sleep. Most of our orthodox sleep is toward the beginning of our sleep period, and most of our REM sleep toward the end. Our body shifts position about 40 times during the night.

How much do we dream?

Everyone dreams every night, but we do not remember most of it. Dreams take up as much as a quarter of your night's sleep. If you wake up in the middle of a dream, you remember it vividly, but if you wake up more than 10 minutes after dreaming, you do not remember anything.

Why do we dream?

According to the psychoanalyst Sigmund Freud, in our dreams we make pictures of and act out things that concern us but of which we are not normally aware. Another theory is that when we dream the brain is sorting through and organizing the day's events.

What would happen if we did not dream?

Although we do not know exactly why we dream, we know it is essential. Someone who is allowed to sleep but is woken up every time she starts to dream soon becomes very confused. Even when she is awake, she may become confused and see things that are not there.

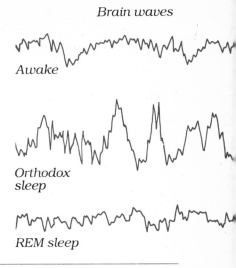

The pattern of brain waves produced by an encephalograph shows the difference in the brain's activity when people are asleep. The pattern also tells researchers when a person goes into either orthodox or REM sleep.

Brain waves

Awake

Orthodox sleep

REM sleep

What is insomnia?

People with insomnia have difficulty sleeping. They find they cannot get to sleep, or cannot stay asleep, even though they are tired. Some people have trouble getting to sleep only occasionally, but for others it can be a regular problem.

What causes insomnia?

A common cause of insomnia is anxiety. People worry about their work, friendships, family, or even about not being able to get to sleep. It can also be difficult to sleep if the bedroom is too hot or too cold, or there is a lack of fresh air in the room. Eating just before going to bed, or drinking tea or coffee (both contain caffeine, which can keep you awake) can also cause insomnia. Some people who do not exercise enough also have trouble sleeping.

Who sleeps the least?

Some people are victims of a very rare condition called total insomnia. These people have been known to go without sleep for many years.

What is daydreaming?

When people's attention wanders and they go into a dreamlike state while they are awake, they are daydreaming. Researchers have found that most, if not all, people daydream. Some daydreams are anxious, centered on a fear of failure, but most of our daydreams are happy and positive.

Perception

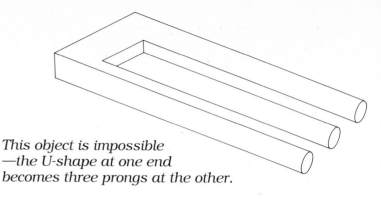

What is perception?

Our brain is bombarded with information about the world around us. Perception is how we interpret this information. For example, when we see a wooden box in front of us, our eyes detect an arrangement of shapes and colors. Using this information, added to our past experience, we then interpret this image as a box of a particular shape, size, and distance.

What is an optical illusion?

An optical illusion is an image that your brain interprets wrongly or strangely. For example, when you see a full moon low on the horizon, it appears to be much larger than when it is high in the sky. But if you measured its apparent size with a ruler held at arm's length, you would see that it is the same in both cases.

How do illusions work?

Illusions occur because of the way your eyes and brain work things out. Your brain has to sort out and make sense of the thousands of signals it receives from your eyes. To do this it compares the signals it receives with what it knows about the world from experience. To try to make the new information fit in with what it already knows, the brain might change the image, so you do not see things exactly as they are.

This object is impossible —the U-shape at one end becomes three prongs at the other.

What is an impossible object?

An impossible object is a type of optical illusion where one part of the picture fools us into interpreting it one way and another part fools us into interpreting it another way. When we try to fit the two together, we cannot do it—we end up with an impossible object.

What is an ambiguous illusion?

Some optical illusions are open to more than one interpretation. For example, is the picture below left of a young woman or an old lady? Your brain cannot decide, so you see first one image and then the other.

When are identical lines different lengths?

Identical straight lines appear to be different lengths when they are framed by two sloping lines. The line at the top seems longer because it appears to be farther away. This is the Ponzo illusion. It relies on the fact that when you see parallel lines such as railroad tracks disappear into the distance, they seem to get closer.

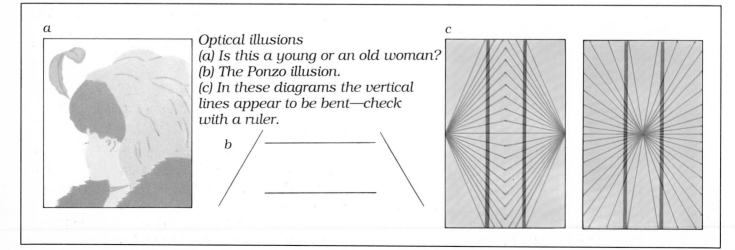

Optical illusions
(a) Is this a young or an old woman?
(b) The Ponzo illusion.
(c) In these diagrams the vertical lines appear to be bent—check with a ruler.

Mental Health

What is mental illness?

Mental illness is illness of the mind. It affects a person's thoughts, feelings, and behavior. A person may become mentally ill when he or she can no longer cope with the stresses of life. But like physical illness, mental illness can often be cured.

What is a mental handicap?

A mental handicap should not be confused with mental illness—it is permanent damage to the brain. The handicap could be due to brain damage or a genetic disorder such as Down's syndrome. Such a condition can never be fully cured, but special education can help the person overcome some of his or her difficulties.

What causes mental illness?

There are many causes of mental illness. Social factors like poor housing, unemployment, family difficulties, or pressures at school or work can result in stress that brings on mental illness. Much mental illness is believed to be caused by an imbalance of chemicals in the brain.

What is the most common mental illness?

Depression is the most common mental illness. A depressed person has feelings of deep sadness and hopelessness and very low self-esteem. Although everyone gets depressed now and then, people suffering from severe depression often cannot eat, sleep, or work properly.

What is a neurosis?

A neurosis is an illness usually brought on by social or emotional factors. People who are suffering from a neurosis may be anxious, or feel insecure or depressed. These feelings happen to everyone, but people with a neurosis may feel them most of the time. This state does not mean that they lose touch with reality.

What is a phobia?

A phobia is a very great fear of some object or situation, such as heights (acrophobia), open spaces (agoraphobia), or enclosed spaces (claustrophobia). The person feels such great terror that the object of her fear stops her from behaving normally or rationally.

Can phobias be cured?

Phobias can usually be cured through behavior therapy. In such therapy the person is gradually made less sensitive to the object of their fear by learning about it and slowly becoming accustomed to its presence. This can take weeks or months of regular treatment.

Arachnophobia is an irrational terror of spiders.

What is a psychosis?

A psychosis is a major disorder of the mind. Psychotic people lose touch with reality. They may hear voices or imagine that everyone is against them (paranoia). Schizophrenia is an example of psychosis.

Does a schizophrenic person have a split personality?

When people think of schizophrenia, they often think of a Jekyll-and-Hyde character—someone with two different personalities. This is not true. Instead, the person tends to be split from reality and may have hallucinations. Some people become aggressive, others are quiet and withdrawn.

HEALTH and MEDICINE

What does it mean to be healthy?

Being healthy is more than not being ill. It is about feeling good in body and mind. If you are in good health, all the organs in your body work together properly and you have the strength and energy to enjoy life to the fullest.

What affects your health?

Your health is affected by almost everything you do, from the food you eat to the amount of exercise you do. Your health is also affected by built-in factors, such as the genes you inherit, your age, and your sex.

What is hygiene?

Hygiene is the science of health and cleanliness. In addition to a balanced diet and plenty of exercise, keeping clean and having regular checkups at the dentist are all essential to staying healthy. Keeping clean helps stop germs from spreading, and looking after your teeth prevents decay.

What is the normal temperature of my body?

Normal body temperature is 98.6°F, although it varies slightly from one person to another. Your body temperature varies slightly throughout the day. Our temperature is lowest in the early hours of the morning and highest at the end of the afternoon. It can go up by as much as four or five degrees when we are ill.

A thermograph is a "heat map" of the body. It shows how, in cold conditions, blood is diverted away from the hands to save body heat.

What does it mean to be physically fit?

Physical fitness is the ability of your whole body, including your muscles, skeleton, heart, and lungs, to work together well to carry out daily activities. Fitness involves three things: strength, flexibility (being able to bend and move easily), and stamina (being able to keep exercising without tiring quickly).

What do we need to do to keep fit?

Fitness experts recommend that we do at least 15 minutes of exercise three times a week to develop a healthy heart and lungs. Swimming, jogging, cycling, and aerobics classes all help develop stamina. If you have a special health problem, you may need to check with your doctor before doing this type of exercise.

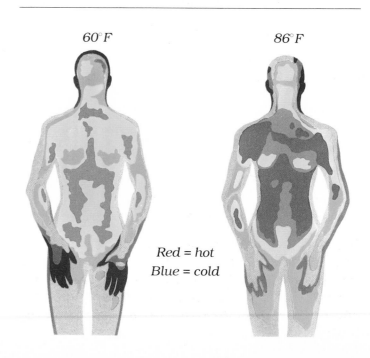

60°F　　*86°F*

Red = hot
Blue = cold

Can too much exercise be bad for you?

Yes. Too much exercise, if you are not used to it, can result in painful injuries such as pulled muscles and strained joints. You should always warm up properly by doing some simple stretching exercises first. If you are not very fit, start gently and build up gradually.

How does the environment affect our health?

There are many environmental factors that affect our health. For example, breathing in pollutants from exhaust fumes every day can result in asthma or other breathing problems. A hot climate can make air pollution worse, causing harmful smog to develop. The conditions we live in will also affect our health.

Thick smog in Los Angeles, California.

Should we take vitamin pills?

A well-balanced diet will give you all the vitamins you need, so a healthy person should not need vitamin pills. However, people who are ill may benefit from some extra vitamins, as may pregnant women or elderly people.

Are too many vitamins bad for you?

In most cases no, but there are some exceptions. Regular large doses of vitamin D (over 100 times the recommended amount) can cause kidney failure. And in a pregnant woman, very large amounts of vitamin A can cause defects in the fetus.

Do children need more vitamins than adults?

Children are active and growing quickly, so they need more of all kinds of foods, not just vitamins. But if they have a well-balanced diet, they do not need vitamin pills.

Which foods should we avoid?

We should cut down on animal fat and salt, since they may both increase the risk of heart disease. Also, too much sugar and fat will make us overweight, making heart disease, kidney problems, and diabetes more likely.

Is fast food bad for you?

Some fast food contains many vitamins and minerals. But many, such as French fries, contain a lot of fat. You should try to eat a variety of fresh foods, especially fruits and vegetables, so that you get the fiber, vitamins, and minerals you need.

Is dieting healthy?

People usually try to lose weight by cutting down on carbohydrates and fats. The problem with a diet is that it lasts only a short time. Afterward people may go back to their old eating habits and put the weight back on. It is much better to get into a routine of eating and exercise that keeps you in shape all the time.

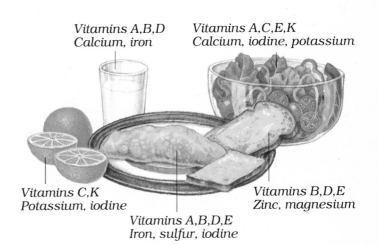

*Vitamins A,B,D
Calcium, iron*

*Vitamins A,C,E,K
Calcium, iodine, potassium*

*Vitamins C,K
Potassium, iodine*

*Vitamins A,B,D,E
Iron, sulfur, iodine*

*Vitamins B,D,E
Zinc, magnesium*

Fresh vegetables, salad, fruits, and dairy products provide many vitamins and minerals.

What is a vegetarian?

A vegetarian is someone who does not eat meat and fish. Most vegetarians eat dairy products, such as eggs and milk, but vegans avoid all animal products. They eat only food that comes from plants.

Is a vegetarian diet healthy?

Yes. A vegetarian diet is often more healthy than a meat-based diet because it includes less fat. Vegans need to take special care, however, to make sure they get enough vitamins B and D and enough protein.

Why should we use a tissue when we sneeze?

When we sneeze, we blast out air and mucus at high speed. The mucus may carry germs that can be passed on to other people when they breathe in. Using a handkerchief keeps these germs to oneself, rather than passing them on.

How can sugar damage your teeth?

Sugar can damage your teeth because the bacteria in your mouth feed on it and turn it into acids. These acids then dissolve small holes in the enamel (the outer surface of your teeth) allowing bacteria to enter. This causes tooth decay.

What is plaque?

Plaque is the sticky stuff that coats your teeth and gums. It is a mixture of saliva, food particles, and bacteria. The bacteria feed on the sugar in plaque, releasing acids that can attack your teeth and gums.

Why is brushing your teeth so important?

Brushing your teeth is important because it helps remove plaque, which causes tooth decay. To get rid of as much plaque as possible, you should brush your teeth after every meal and use dental floss to clean the gaps between your teeth. Using special plaque-disclosing tablets that turn plaque red, you can check how well you brush your teeth.

How is gum disease prevented?

If plaque builds up at the base of the tooth, it can form a hard brown deposit called tartar. Tartar irritates the gums, and they may become inflamed and bleed easily. Careful brushing and flossing stops plaque from building up. Your dentist can scrape tartar off your teeth when you go for a checkup.

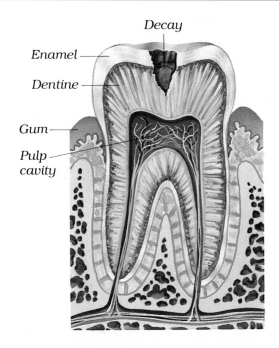

Decay
Enamel
Dentine
Gum
Pulp cavity

If plaque builds up on your teeth, it attacks the enamel, causing decay. If the decay continues, the tooth may need to be filled.

 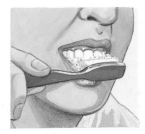

Brushing your teeth after meals and flossing between the teeth will help to keep your teeth and gums healthy.

Why is fluoride put in water?

Fluoride is sometimes put in water supplies because it helps strengthen the enamel in children's teeth.

Disease

What is a disease?

A disease is a condition, other than an injury, which prevents your body from working properly. Diseases have many different causes.

What are signs and symptoms?

Signs and symptoms are the characteristics caused by a disease. A sign is a feature that can be seen or measured when the patient is examined. Skin rashes and a high blood sugar level are examples of signs. A symptom is something a patient feels, but a doctor cannot see or measure. Pain is a symptom.

A rash is an obvious sign of disease, whereas stomach pains are a symptom that the patient describes.

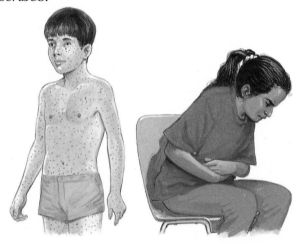

What is a diagnosis?

A diagnosis is the identification of the particular disease that a patient is suffering from. The doctor makes a judgment, which is based on the patient's signs and symptoms, together with his or her knowledge and experience.

What is a microbe?

A microbe, or microorganism, is a living creature that is too small to be seen with the naked eye. Many consist of a single cell.

What causes diseases?

Some diseases are caused by microorganisms entering our body and then feeding and reproducing inside it. In doing so they may damage the body, or poison it by releasing toxic waste substances. Other diseases are caused by faults in one of the body systems.

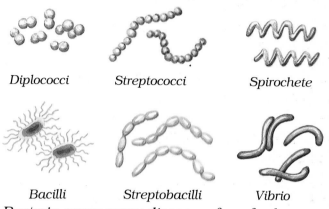

Diplococci   Streptococci   Spirochete

Bacilli   Streptobacilli   Vibrio

Bacteria cause many diseases, from food poisoning to tuberculosis. Some common disease-causing bacteria are shown above.

Which microbes cause disease?

Four main types of microbes cause disease: viruses, bacteria, protozoa, and fungi. Disease-causing microbes are often known as germs.

What are bacteria?

Bacteria are microbes. They are smaller than our body cells. Bacteria are all around us—in the air, in soil, and on our skin.

Which diseases do bacteria cause?

Bacterial diseases include cholera, tetanus, tuberculosis (TB), whooping cough, typhoid, and most kinds of food poisoning.

What is a virus?

Viruses are the smallest living things. Most are more than a thousand times smaller than a period on this page. They are only really alive when they enter the cells of another living creature (organism) and start to multiply inside it. On their own, viruses cannot feed or grow, and show no signs of life.

How do viruses cause disease?

Viruses cause disease by entering cells in our body and taking control of them. They "hijack" the cell and use its resources to make copies of themselves. Eventually the cell bursts and releases the new viruses, which enter other cells and multiply. Tens of thousands of cells are destroyed, causing the disease symptoms.

Are viruses dangerous?

Viruses can be very dangerous. The polio virus destroys skeletal muscles and causes paralysis. It is believed that the HIV virus leads to AIDS. The problem with most viruses is that there aren't any drugs that are effective against them. You recover from a viral disease only when your immune system beats the virus. This is how you recover from less serious viral infections such as common colds and flu.

Which diseases do protozoa cause?

Protozoa are single-celled animals common in water and soil. They are larger than bacteria. Malaria, sleeping sickness, and some kinds of dysentery are caused by protozoa.

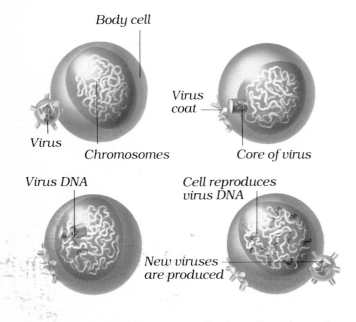

Body cell

Virus coat

Virus

Chromosomes

Core of virus

Virus DNA

Cell reproduces virus DNA

New viruses are produced

Viruses inject DNA into our body cells. The cells then make hundreds of copies of the virus, which infect and destroy other cells in turn.

How are diseases spread?

Germs, or pathogens, are spread in many ways. The viruses that cause colds and flu are spread in droplets of saliva coughed, sneezed, or breathed out by an infected person. Some diseases are spread in food and drink, such as the food poisoning bacteria *Salmonella*. Some animals carry diseases that they spread to people. For example, the fleas of black rats carried the germ responsible for the plague in Europe in the Middle Ages.

What is an infectious disease?

An infectious disease is a disease caused by a microbe that can be passed on to someone else. Non-infectious diseases such as cancer, diabetes, and vitamin deficiency diseases cannot be passed on.

What is a contagious disease?

A contagious disease is a disease in which the disease-causing microbe must be passed from one person to another by direct contact with the person's tissues or fluids. It cannot live outside the body. One example is ringworm, a skin infection caused by a fungus, which is commonly transmitted by direct contact.

Why don't we get diseases more often?

Every day we are in contact with millions of bacteria. The reason we do not get ill more often is that most of them are harmless. We also have very effective barriers to stop germs from getting into our bodies and various mechanisms for knocking out any that do get past our defenses.

How do germs get inside our bodies?

Germs can get inside our bodies through openings such as the nose and mouth when we breathe in. These openings are lined with moist membranes that act as protective barriers, but they also provide ideal conditions for germs to grow. The germs can then infect other organs. We swallow germs with our food and drink. Some germs can also get into the body if the skin is damaged.

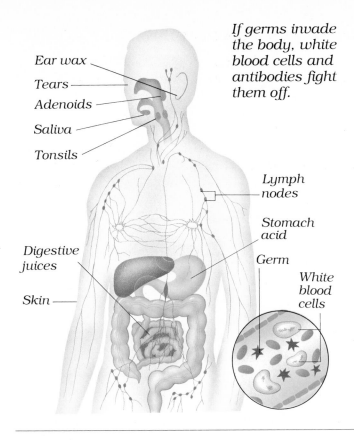

Ear wax
Tears
Adenoids
Saliva
Tonsils

If germs invade the body, white blood cells and antibodies fight them off.

Lymph nodes
Stomach acid
Germ
White blood cells
Digestive juices
Skin

How do our bodies deal with germs?

Our bodies have various ways of dealing with germs. If the skin is damaged, a blood clot will seal up the cut. The nose, mouth, air passages, and small intestine are all lined with mucus, which stops germs from getting through. Tears and sweat kill germs with chemicals, and strong acid in the stomach kills most germs in our food.

What is our immune system?

Our immune system is our defense against infection. Two kinds of white blood cells react and neutralize harmful germs. Lymphocytes produce antibodies that defeat the germs, and phagocytes eat them.

What are antibodies?

Antibodies are chemicals that stop germs from multiplying or slow them down so they can be eaten by phagocytes. Once the lymphocytes have defeated a germ, they "remember" which antibody killed it. The next time they meet the germ, they can quickly make the correct antibody. This is how we become immune to a disease.

What is the lymphatic system?

The lymphatic, or lymph, system is a network of thin tubes that contain a liquid called lymph. One of the main functions of lymph is to help the body fight disease. At intervals along the lymph system are small, bean-like swellings called lymph nodes. This is where the lymphocytes that fight infection are stored.

What are the stages of a disease?

There are normally four stages of a disease. In a viral infection such as a cold, the first stage is infection, when the virus enters the body and gets past its defenses. The second stage is the incubation period, when the virus multiplies itself. During this stage you may be able to infect other people. The third stage, or peak, is when the telltale signs and symptoms develop. The fourth stage is recovery, when the immune system defeats the disease.

Do insects cause disease?

Although very few insects cause disease directly, many carry diseases. Some of the world's most serious diseases are spread by insects: malaria by the mosquito; plague by the flea; sleeping sickness by the tsetse fly; and cholera, polio, and dysentery by the housefly.

Certain insects are vectors, which means that they carry organisms that cause disease.

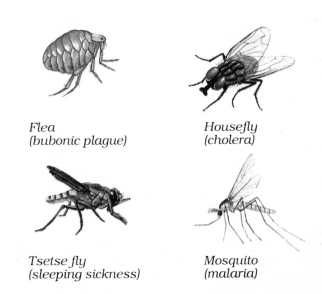

Flea
(bubonic plague)

Housefly
(cholera)

Tsetse fly
(sleeping sickness)

Mosquito
(malaria)

History of Medicine

Who was the first doctor?

The first doctor known by name was Imhotep, an ancient Egyptian who lived about 2650 B.C. After his death the Egyptians worshiped him as a god for his healing powers.

Who was the "Father of Medicine"?

Hippocrates, a Greek doctor who lived in the 4th century B.C., is sometimes called the "Father of Western Medicine." He knew the importance of hygiene and a good diet, and he helped develop medicine as a science based on careful observation and record-keeping. He is believed to have written the Hippocratic oath, which states rules that a doctor should follow. Until quite recently, all doctors had to swear to keep this oath.

Who was Galen?

Galen (A.D.129–199) was the most famous doctor in the Roman world. He was a surgeon at a school for gladiators, where he learned much about the body's structure. Galen developed his knowledge by dissecting animals. He later became physician to three Roman emperors.

Who was Avicenna?

Avicenna (980–1037) was an important doctor in the medieval Islamic world. He wrote a *Canon of Medicine*, which combined his own medical knowledge with the discoveries of Roman and Arabic medicine. Avicenna's theory and methods were taught in Europe for 700 years.

Who was Vesalius?

Vesalius (1514–1564) was the first person to make detailed observations based on the dissection of human bodies. He got his supply of bodies from recent graves. Vesalius studied medicine in Belgium before becoming a professor of anatomy in Italy at the age of 24. In 1543 he published a textbook on the structure of the human body. He showed that many of Galen's findings, dating from 1,400 years before, were inaccurate.

Who led the way in public health?

Sewage systems were built in Mesopotamia and the Indus Valley as early as 1500 B.C. The ancient Romans also realized that dirt and overcrowding spread disease. In the sixth century B.C., Rome had a system of underground sewers to carry away waste. Soon afterward, huge aqueducts were constructed to bring in fresh water. Most Roman towns and cities had their own public baths.

A small public bath in a Roman town.

What did William Harvey discover?

William Harvey (1578–1657) was an English doctor. By making observations and performing simple experiments, he showed that the heart pumps blood around the body in one direction in a continuous loop. One of his most famous experiments is still demonstrated by medical teachers today.

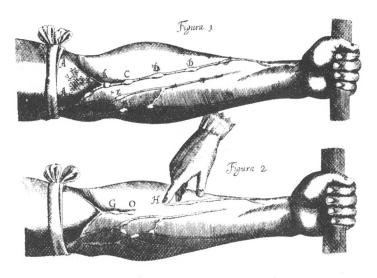

Harvey's experiment: if a cloth is tied tightly around the arm, the veins will bulge out. Lumps in the vein show the position of the valves. If one of the veins is pressed behind the valve, the blood drains out of it, but it cannot fill up again.

Who discovered vaccination?

Vaccination originated in China in the tenth century B.C. Lady Mary Wortley Montagu introduced vaccination against smallpox into Britain in 1771, but the best-known demonstration was by Edward Jenner in 1796. Jenner vaccinated a boy with fluid from a milkmaid's cowpox blister; the boy caught cowpox, a disease similar to smallpox, but milder. When the boy was later inoculated with smallpox, he did not develop it.

Who first realized that laughing gas was an anesthetic?

In 1799 Humphry Davy, an English chemist, made the accidental discovery that "laughing gas," or nitrous oxide, could ease pain. It would keep a patient conscious, but laughing.

Which dentist first used ether?

In 1846 William Morton, an American dentist, was the first to give his patients ether as an anesthetic.

What is Florence Nightingale famous for?

Florence Nightingale (1820–1910) was an English woman who is famous for her pioneering efforts to make nursing a respected profession. During the Crimean War (1853–1856) she led a team of nurses who cared for injured British troops. She vastly improved the conditions of hygiene and cleanliness for hospitalized soldiers.

Who discovered that germs cause disease?

Louis Pasteur (1822–1895), a French professor of chemistry, demonstrated that germs enter wounds and cause disease. He proved that germs did not simply grow out of the wound, as had been thought previously.

Louis Pasteur invented pasteurization, a process that kills harmful bacteria in food.

What is pasteurization?

Pasteurization is the process of rapidly heating and cooling a liquid to kill harmful bacteria. It is named after Louis Pasteur, who first used this method to prevent wine from going bad. It is now used to prolong the shelf life of milk.

Which disease became extinct in the 1970s?

Smallpox was declared extinct by the World Health Organization on May 8, 1980. Global vaccination programs led to the eradication of the disease.

Modern Medicine

Why do the staff in operating rooms wear gowns and masks?

Gowns and masks prevent bacteria and other germs from traveling from the body or clothes of the staff into the patient's wound during the operation. Other precautions are also taken. The clothes the staff wear are sterilized so they are completely free of bacteria. The whole operating room itself is a sterile environment—even the air is cleaned to remove bacteria.

Why do people have operations?

Usually operations involve cutting into the body, to remove damaged or diseased tissues, such as someone's tonsils or appendix. Exploratory operations are performed so that the surgeon can find out what is wrong with the patient. Some operations are carried out to replace body parts with artificial ones, such as a hip or a heart valve. Emergency operations may save someone's life if, for example, the patient has had a serious accident.

Operating rooms are kept as sterile as possible to prevent infection. Staff wear gowns and masks, and even the air is sterile.

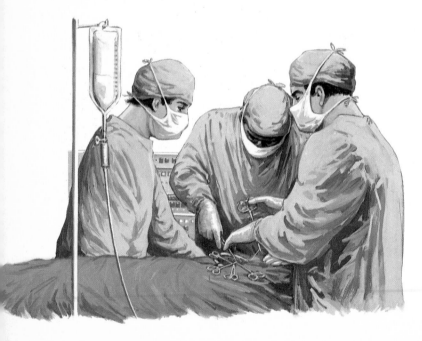

What does an anesthetist do?

An anesthetist specializes in giving patients drugs that make them either unconscious or insensitive to pain during an operation. An anesthetic is given by injection just before the operation. If a further anesthetic is needed during the operation it can be inhaled as a gas. The anesthetist also carefully monitors the patient's breathing and heartbeat.

What are antibiotics?

Antibiotics are drugs that are used to kill bacteria or stop them from reproducing inside the body. Antibiotics are taken as tablets or by injection. Most antibiotics come from molds. Penicillin is the best-known example.

What are antiseptics?

Antiseptics are chemicals that kill microbes or slow down their growth. They are used to clean wounds and sometimes to help treat mouth or throat infections. Many antiseptics are poisonous and can be used only externally.

What is an endoscope used for?

An endoscope is a device that allows a surgeon to examine internal organs, take samples, or even perform operations without making a large cut in the patient's body. It consists of a thin flexible tube containing glass fibers that send light down the tube and carry the image back to the doctor's eye. Instruments for sampling or cutting tissues can be operated by wires traveling down the tube.

How do X rays work?

X rays are invisible waves of energy that can pass through soft tissues like skin and muscle but are stopped by heavier tissue such as bone. Passing X rays through the body and onto a light-sensitive plate produces an image that can show damage such as broken bones. Where X rays pass through the body, the plate is blackened; where they do not, the plate remains light. In addition to bone damage or disease, fluid on a lung can be detected.

What is a CAT scan?

CAT stands for Computerized Axial Tomography, an X ray technique that takes photographs of slices through a patient's body. The X ray source is rotated around the patient so that he is scanned from all sides. A CAT scanner shows soft tissues as well as bones. Using a series of images, a computer generates a three-dimensional picture of the body.

Scanner

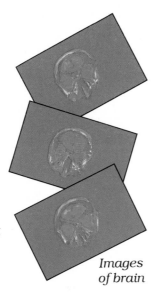

During a CAT scan, X rays are fired through the body at different angles. A computer compiles the images to generate a picture showing a "slice" through the body.

Images of brain

How is radio used to see inside patients?

NMR, short for Nuclear Magnetic Resonance, is a scanning technique that uses radio waves instead of X rays. When the patient is placed inside a magnetic field, tiny electrical signals are produced. The signals change depending on whether an organ is healthy or not. The NMR technique can be used in cases where X rays might be harmful.

What is a PET scan?

Positron Emission Tomography, or a PET scan, detects the amount of activity in different parts of the body. A radioactive substance is injected into the bloodstream and collects in certain parts of the body. Radiation counts are highest in these areas. This can show the position of, say, a tumor, which is displayed on a computer screen.

What is ultrasound used for?

Ultrasound is high frequency sound that cannot be heard but can be used to look inside a patient's body. Sound waves are directed into the body and reflected back from internal structures as an echo. The echo is picked up by a receiver, which produces an image on a screen. Ultrasound is used to check the health of a fetus inside the mother.

How can sound be used to destroy things?

If a soprano singer hits just the right high note, the sound waves can cause a glass to vibrate and shatter. This principle is used to destroy kidney stones. Kidney stones are deposits of calcium salts that sometimes build up inside the kidney. Sound waves are focused on the precise point where the stone lies. Up to 2,000 shock waves are given over one hour. The tiny fragments of the broken kidney stone later leave the body in the urine.

What is amputation?

Amputation is the removal of a limb or part of a limb. This may be done if the limb has been damaged beyond repair or if it has a dangerous infection that cannot be treated and could spread to other parts of the body.

This man has had his right leg amputated, but he still enjoys the challenge of skiing.

Can doctors sew severed limbs back on?

Doctors can sometimes sew on part of a severed limb within a few hours if it has been preserved in ice. The surgery is extremely delicate. It is performed using a microscope, tiny surgical instruments, needles, and thread. Nerve fibers, veins, and arteries all have to be joined back together. Stitching a hand back on can take 19 hours. It takes over a year before the person can use his hand almost normally.

How do surgeons use lasers?

Since the mid-1960s lasers have been used in certain operations to burn away tissue with minimum damage. At the same time, blood vessels are sealed to stop them from bleeding. The laser beam contains a great deal of energy that is directed down an optical fiber, and can be used in an endoscope. Lasers can be used in delicate eye surgery, to cut away certain cancers, seal stomach ulcers, and remove birthmarks.

Who would need intensive care?

People who have just had a major operation or are seriously ill need intensive care to help them recover. If the patient is unconscious, she may be fed intravenously. Food and water are passed through a tube inserted into her arm. Her heart rate is carefully monitored, and she may need a respirator to help her breathe.

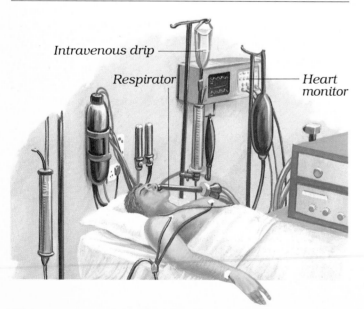

Intravenous drip

Respirator

Heart monitor

What is a transplant?

A transplant operation is the removal of a diseased organ or tissue from a patient, and its replacement with a healthy one from a donor.

Which body parts can be transplanted?

The first parts of the body to be transplanted were the kidneys, cornea, and bone marrow. The first human heart transplant was performed by Dr. Christiaan Barnard in 1967. Today, heart, liver, lung, pancreas, and bowel transplants are all possible.

Which body parts can be replaced with artificial ones?

A whole range of artificial parts are now available to replace existing tissues that are damaged or diseased. These include artificial heart pacemakers and valves, blood vessels, and various joints, such as the hip and knee.

How can radiation be used to treat cancer?

X rays or gamma radiation can be used to treat certain forms of cancer. Body cells are most susceptible to radiation damage when they are dividing. Because cancerous cells multiply rapidly, they are more prone to radiation damage than the surrounding healthy tissues. Treatment is carefully controlled, but there may be side effects such as hair loss and nausea.

What is genetic engineering?

Genetic engineering is the process of adding, removing, or transferring individual genes. Much of this work is done using bacteria and viruses. These microbes are simpler to study, and are able to receive individual genes more easily than other organisms. Human genes can be inserted into microbes. The gene then makes the microbes produce a particular substance that can be extracted and used. Insulin, used for treating diabetes, is produced in this way.

An intensive-care unit monitors a patient's condition after a serious operation.

Drugs

What is a drug?

A drug is a chemical substance that alters the way your mind or body works. Many drugs are in everyday use as medicines, either by prescription from a doctor or for sale "over the counter." Some drugs, such as heroin and cocaine, are illegal.

Medical drugs can be swallowed, inhaled, or injected. Some can be absorbed through the skin.

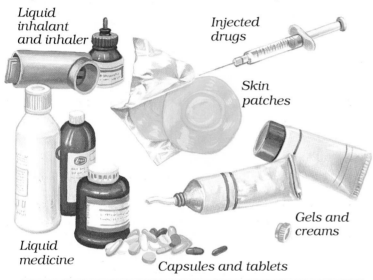

Liquid inhalant and inhaler

Injected drugs

Skin patches

Liquid medicine

Gels and creams

Capsules and tablets

What is a stimulant?

Stimulants are drugs that speed up the actions of parts of the nervous system. They make a person feel more alert. Their effect is similar to that of the hormone adrenaline. Stimulants can be habit-forming, and illegal stimulants, such as amphetamine or cocaine, are dangerous. They can cause paranoia and may lead to personality problems and even death.

What does a sedative do?

Sedatives, or depressants, slow down parts of the nervous system. Some have the effect of relieving anxiety and making the patient feel relaxed. Some, such as barbiturates and other tranquilizers, are used to help people sleep. However, one can become addicted to, or physically dependent on, them.

Where do drugs come from?

Many drugs are made artificially in laboratories. Some are based on substances found in plants and herbs with healing properties. Digitalis, for example, a substance found in foxglove leaves, slows down heart rate and is used in the treatment of heart disease. Some drugs, such as the antibiotic penicillin, are made from fungi. Others are made by genetic engineering.

What kind of drug is nicotine?

Nicotine, a drug in tobacco, is a stimulant. In small doses it can make a person feel relaxed. It speeds up the pulse rate and raises blood pressure. It is, in fact, poisonous and addictive and can cause heart and breathing problems.

How are medical drugs discovered?

New and useful drugs are still discovered each year in plants. More frequently, however, drugs are produced artificially in laboratories by pharmaceutical companies. Researchers use up-to-date chemical and computer technology to analyze drugs. They make hundreds of similar chemicals, in the hope that a few of them may be more effective against a particular disease, or cause fewer side effects.

Scientists work under strictly controlled laboratory conditions when developing new drugs. This researcher is working with metals to develop new medical compounds.

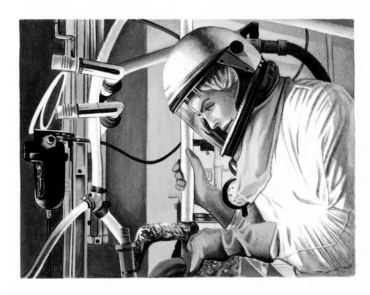

How are medical drugs tested?

Drugs are carefully tested on animal tissue cultures in glass containers and also on live animals. If they prove suitable, they may be tested on human tissue cultures. There is pressure to avoid experimenting on live animals, since many people feel that is very cruel.

What are clinical trials?

Clinical trials are tests to see whether a drug is both useful and safe for humans without any harmful side effects. After being tested first on tissue cultures and, possibly, on laboratory animals, the drugs are then tried out on healthy volunteers. The drug is then given to volunteers who have the disease or disorder that the drug has been developed to treat.

A new drug developed to treat breathing problems is being tested on this asthma sufferer.

What is meant by drug abuse?

Someone who abuses drugs takes them for a purpose for which they were not originally intended, or in amounts that are dangerous. The drug is usually taken for the pleasurable effects it gives, or as a way of escaping from problems in everyday life. An abuser may become addicted to the drug. He will then suffer withdrawal symptoms such as muscle cramps, headaches, and shivering when he stops taking it. This is because his body has gotten used to the drug being present.

Does coffee contain a drug?

Yes. Coffee, tea, and some soft drinks contain the drug caffeine. As this is a mild stimulant, it reduces tension and increases mental alertness. But, like other stimulants, it is habit-forming. Large amounts taken regularly increase the chances of getting heart and circulatory disorders.

Is alcohol a drug?

Alcohol is a drug that acts as a sedative. In small amounts it can produce a feeling of well-being. But in larger amounts it affects the drinker's judgment, coordination, and behavior. Alcohol has a number of damaging effects. It kills brain cells and irritates the lining of the stomach. Over time, it may lead to liver and heart disease. Both of these can be fatal. Alcohol is one of the most widely abused substances.

Why do athletes undergo drug tests?

Many drugs are banned by sporting organizations because they can unfairly improve an athlete's performance. For example, the drugs called anabolic steroids can improve strength by increasing muscle size. Amphetamines increase alertness, stimulate the whole body to produce extra effort, and stave off exhaustion. Both these types of drugs are banned. Taking them is not only cheating, but can seriously damage the athlete's health.

What is aspirin?

Aspirin and paracetamol are mild painkillers, or analgesics. They are used to combat headaches and fever. Aspirin also reduces swelling and inflammation. Both aspirin and paracetamol are dangerous if used incorrectly.

What is quinine?

Quinine, a chemical obtained from the bark of the cinchona tree in South America, was the first effective drug used against the malaria parasite. It is also thought to be the first drug that was used to treat the cause of a disease rather than its symptoms.

Alternative Medicine

What is alternative medicine?

Alternative, or holistic, medicine is a type of treatment not usually given by family doctors. Alternative medical treatments often involve treating the person as a whole, instead of treating a specific condition or symptom.

What is homeopathy?

Homeopathy is a system of treatment using tiny quantities of chemical and herbal remedies. It is based on the principle that the signs and symptoms of illness are caused by the body fighting the disease and not by the illness itself.

What is acupuncture?

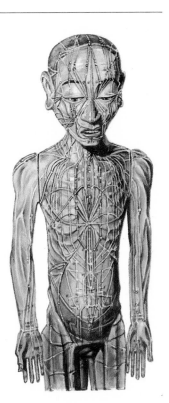

Acupuncture is a form of ancient Chinese treatment based on the idea that energy flows through the body in channels called meridians. Disease or pain occurs where the flow of energy is blocked. To unblock the flow, an acupuncturist inserts needles in various parts of the body. This does not hurt and gives relief in many cases.

This seventeenth-century Chinese study figure shows the meridians used in acupuncture.

What else is acupuncture used for?

Acupuncture is widely used in China as an anesthetic. In the last 30 years, over one million operations have been successfully carried out using needles instead of chemical anesthetics.

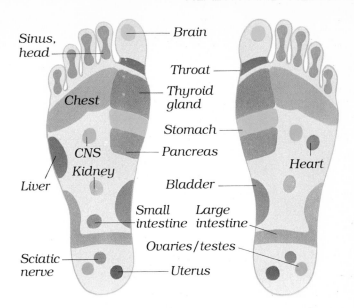

Like acupuncture, reflexology is based on the belief that illness is caused by blocked channels of energy. Areas of the feet, which relate to different organs, are massaged to unblock these channels.

What is hypnotherapy used for?

Hypnotherapy may be used to treat an emotional problem, a harmful habit, or even a physical problem. It is particularly useful in helping to relieve stress and treating some types of addiction. The therapist asks the patient about her situation in order to make a diagnosis. In later sessions, the therapist uses hypnosis to work with the person's subconscious mind and develop ways to help solve her problems.

What is osteopathy?

Osteopathy uses manipulation, massage, and exercise to treat various disorders, usually of the bones and muscles. Many people go to an osteopath if they have "thrown out" their back. They are treated by a simple manipulation of the spine.

How can massage improve your health?

Massage involves rubbing, manipulating, or kneading parts of the body. Massage is helpful in relieving physical and mental stress, headaches, backaches, and arthritis. Massage is also useful in helping patients recover from more serious conditions, such as heart surgery.

WHO?

Who was Sigmund Freud?

Sigmund Freud was an Austrian doctor who developed psychoanalysis in the 1890s. Psychoanalysis is a way of treating mental illness. The doctor asks the patient questions and gradually helps the patient understand the reasons for his or her state of mind.

Who was Elizabeth Blackwell?

She was the first woman in the world to qualify as a doctor, in the United States in 1849.

Who first used X rays to look inside the human body?

Wilhelm Roentgen took the first X-ray pictures, of the bones in his wife's hands, in 1895.

Who was Alexis St. Martin?

Alexis was an 18-year-old who was wounded in a shotgun accident in the 1820s. The wound healed, leaving a flap of skin covering a hole in his stomach. A doctor was therefore able to carry out research into digestion by examining the contents of Alexis's stomach.

Who was the oldest woman to give birth?

Ruth Kisler of Oregon gave birth to a daughter in 1956 at age 57.

Who had the most children?

Mrs. Vassilyev, a peasant in eighteenth-century Russia, gave birth to 69 children in all: 16 pairs of twins, 7 sets of triplets, and 4 sets of quadruplets.

Who was Gregor Mendel?

Gregor Mendel was an Austrian monk and avid plant grower. In the 1850s and 1860s, he pioneered work on genetics—the inheritance of characteristics—by performing breeding experiments with pea plants.

Who first used a microscope?

The microscope was invented toward the end of the sixteenth century by the Dutch optician Hans Jansen, with the help of his son Zacharias.

Who first used antiseptics in surgery?

In 1865, Joseph Lister, professor of surgery in Glasgow, Scotland, used carbolic acid as an antiseptic in operations. It was used as a spray to sterilize the patient's wound, the surgeon's hands, the operating instruments, and the air around the patient.

Who discovered viruses?

Viruses were discovered by Dmitry Ivanovsky, a Russian scientist, in 1892.

Who was Asclepius?

Asclepius was a successful doctor in ancient Greece. According to legend he was killed by the jealous god Zeus. Later, the Greeks worshiped Asclepius as the god of healing, and temples were built in his name and used as hospitals.

Who first used sound to "see" inside a body?

The American physician Robert Lee Wild was the first person to use sound reflections to "see" inside the body, in 1952.

Who discovered cells?

Although scientists using early microscopes had observed cells, they did not know what they were. Robert Hooke, a British scientist, was the first person to give them a name.

Who gets prickly heat?

People who sweat a lot may suffer from prickly heat. It is an irritating skin rash that can develop in areas where sweat collects.

Who was Herophilus?

Herophilus was a doctor in ancient Greece who founded the first school of anatomy around 300 B.C.

Who was Alderotti?

Taddeo Alderotti was a thirteenth-century Italian doctor. He encouraged other physicians to read and learn from the discoveries of the ancient Greeks, such as Hippocrates.

Who was Chen Ch'uan?

Chen Ch'uan was a Chinese doctor who died in A.D. 643. He was the first person to note the symptoms of diabetes.

Who were Banting and Best?

Frederick Banting and Charles Best were the Canadian scientists who in 1921 discovered insulin, the hormone that controls blood glucose levels. With the help of J. B. Collip, a chemist, they purified extracts of insulin and used them to treat diabetic patients.

Who invented the stethoscope?

The stethoscope was invented in 1814 by René Laennec, a French doctor. His version was made from paper, rolled to form a cone.

Who developed a vaccine for polio?

A vaccine for polio was developed by American scientist Jonas Salk in 1954. As a result of his work, polio was practically eradicated in Western nations.

Who suffers from jet lag?

Travelers who cross from one time zone to another may suffer from jet lag—disturbed sleep and activity patterns—as a result. For example, a business traveler on a journey from Portugal to the west coast of America (which is eight hours behind) may feel it is time to go to bed, even though it is only the afternoon, local time.

Who might get the bends?

A diver returning from deep water to the surface too quickly may get the bends. The bends are pains and tissue damage caused by bubbles of nitrogen or helium forming in the blood or being trapped in the joints.

Who makes a prognosis?

A doctor makes a prognosis—it is the doctor's opinion of the likely outcome of a disease.

Who practiced ayurveda?

Ayurveda, a form of medicine, was practiced by the peoples of ancient India. It stressed the prevention as well as the treatment of illness and developed an impressive knowledge of drugs, and some knowledge of surgery.

Who suffers from golfer's elbow?

Anyone who overuses the muscles of the wrist and fingers can suffer from golfer's elbow—it is tenderness and pain on the inside of the elbow and forearm.

Who is Doctor Spock?

Dr. Benjamin Spock is a noted child care expert. In 1946 he advised parents to have a more relaxed approach to raising their children. His ideas were extremely influential.

Who receives prenatal care?

A pregnant woman receives prenatal care. It is designed to monitor the health of the woman and the fetus, and helps prepare the mother for childbirth.

Who was Ambroise Paré?

Ambroise Paré was a sixteenth-century French military surgeon. He was the first person to treat injuries by stemming the bleeding instead of burning the wound. He used soothing lotions, not boiling oil, to clean wounds.

Who gets SAD?

People who become very depressed in winter get SAD—short for Seasonal Affective Disorder. It is believed to be caused by lack of sunlight.

Who was Alexander Fleming?

Alexander Fleming was a Scottish scientist who discovered the antibiotic penicillin in 1928.

WHAT?

What is an organism?

An organism is a living thing. Animals and plants are organisms. So are microbes, which you can see only with a microscope.

What is a species?

A species is a particular kind of organism. We belong to the human species, the Latin name for which is *Homo sapiens*, meaning "wise man."

What do living things have in common?

All living organisms show seven basic activities. They grow, reproduce, and feed. They show movement and are sensitive to their surroundings. They also get energy from food (respiration) and get rid of waste (excretion).

What causes a mutation in a cell?

Mutations are caused by mistakes that occur naturally when cells divide, but they are quite rare. The likelihood of mutation can be increased by exposure to certain types of radiation, such as X rays.

What is carotene?

Carotene is an orange pigment found in some foods, such as carrots. The body converts carotene into vitamin A, which is needed for good night vision and healthy skin.

What is a spinal tap?

A spinal tap is performed when a hollow needle is inserted into the lower spine to extract spinal fluid for examination or to inject types of drugs.

What is a birthmark?

A birthmark is a blemish on the skin that has been there from birth. Birthmarks are caused by extra blood vessels or pigment in a certain area of skin.

What causes burping?

Your stomach often contains air or gas from swallowing air or from gas in fizzy drinks. The entrance valve to the stomach may suddenly open, releasing the gas. The gas then vibrates in the throat, making a burping sound.

What is glue ear?

Glue ear is a blockage caused by repeated infection of the middle ear. A sticky fluid forms that stops the eardrum and three tiny ear bones from vibrating freely. Glue ear results in slight deafness and pain.

What is ESP?

ESP (extrasensory perception) is the ability to gather information without apparently using the five senses — sight, sound, touch, taste, or smell. Information is gathered by a "sixth sense."

What types of ESP are there?

There are three types. Clairvoyance is the ability to sense things happening at a distance, maybe many miles away. Telepathy is transferring thoughts from one person to another. Precognition is predicting future events.

What evidence is there for ESP?

There is some scientific evidence of clairvoyance and telepathy in a few people. However, much of the evidence comes from word-of-mouth rather than proper scientific investigation.

What is a concussion?

When someone loses consciousness for a short time after receiving a blow to the head, they are said to have a concussion. The loss of consciousness is caused by the brain being jarred and its electrical activity being upset.

What is the kiss of life?

The kiss of life is another name for mouth-to-mouth resuscitation. It involves blowing into a person's mouth to keep air moving in and out of their lungs if they have stopped breathing.

What causes hay fever?

Hay fever is caused by dust or pollen irritating the lining of the nose. In some people this triggers an allergic reaction, causing cells in the nose to release histamine. Histamine produces a runny nose, sneezing, and red, watery eyes.

What is eczema?

There are several types of eczema or dermatitis. In all types the skin is itchy, red, and flaky and may have blisters.

What is meningitis?

Meningitis is an infection of the meninges, the membranes around the brain and spinal cord.

What is brainwashing?

Brainwashing is a way of putting new ideas into someone's head, and getting rid of old ones, by subjecting a person to great mental pressure. Techniques include depriving the person of sleep or threatening them physically.

What is halitosis?

Halitosis is another name for bad breath. Tooth decay or sinus problems can cause bad breath.

What causes senility?

Senility is a decline in mental ability with old age. Two main causes are Alzheimer's disease, in which the brain tissue withers, and strokes, which cut off blood supply to parts of the brain.

What are food additives?

Food additives include colorings, preservatives, and chemicals that change the natural texture or flavor of food.

What is anorexia?

Anorexia nervosa is an eating disorder that usually affects young girls. Anorexics refuse to eat enough food, often in the belief that they are too fat. They lose so much weight that their bodies fail to function properly.

What is bulimia?

Bulimia nervosa is an eating disorder related to anorexia. A person who suffers from bulimia has bouts of excessive eating and then tries to control her weight by making herself vomit afterward.

What is an impacted wisdom tooth?

When a wisdom tooth is wedged against the tooth next to it, we say it is impacted. This happens because the jaw is so crowded that the wisdom teeth cannot grow properly. An impacted tooth can hurt and may need to be removed.

What are false teeth made of?

A set of false teeth, or a denture, is usually made out of plastic.

What is food poisoning?

The most common form of food poisoning is caused by harmful bacteria such as *Salmonella*, which can get into your food. The germs multiply and produce poisons (toxins) that make you ill. The main signs of food poisoning are pains in the abdomen, vomiting, and diarrhea.

What is a urine test for?

The most common urine test is for the presence of sugars, which may indicate diabetes. A urine test will also show if a woman is pregnant.

What is anatomy?

Anatomy is the scientific study of the physical structure of the body.

What is physiology?

Physiology is the science concerned with the processes that take place inside the body.

What is an anticoagulant?

An anticoagulant is a drug that stops the blood from clotting, or coagulating. For example, blood used for transfusions has citric acid added as an anticoagulant.

What is an allergy?

An allergy occurs when people react to an object or chemical as though it were a germ. They release antibodies to combat the irritation, and the affected cells release histamine. This produces the signs and symptoms of the allergy.

What is the difference between a tickle and an itch?

Both are irritating sensations that trigger touch and pain receptors in the skin. If the sensation moves, it is a tickle; an itch stays in one place.

What are tonsils for?

The tonsils guard against harmful bacteria entering the throat. They are part of the lymphatic system and contain white blood cells that attack bacteria.

What is tonsillitis?

Tonsillitis is an infection of the tonsils. If the tonsils become infected repeatedly, they can be removed surgically without causing any harm.

What are Siamese twins?

They are identical twins that are born attached to one another by a part of the body. Sometimes it is possible to separate them with an operation.

What is hypothermia?

Hypothermia is the lowering of a person's body temperature to a dangerous level. Tiredness, muscle stiffness, confusion, and ultimately death can result.

What is plastic surgery?

Plastic surgery is any operation that is carried out to repair or reconstruct skin and the tissues underneath. It does not usually involve plastic.

What is a parasite?

A parasite is an organism that lives on, or in, another organism. It feeds off it and causes it harm in some way, however small.

What does AIDS stand for?

AIDS stands for Acquired Immune Deficiency Syndrome. AIDS is a fatal disease thought to be caused by a virus known as HIV. This virus attacks people's immune systems so they cannot defend themselves against other diseases.

What is interferon?

Interferon is one of the few substances produced by body cells to attack viruses.

What is chiropractic?

Chiropractic is a form of alternative medicine. It is based on the belief that the main cause of illness is misalignment of the spine and surrounding tissues. Treatment involves pressing on the back and manipulating the spine.

What does a physiotherapist do?

A physiotherapist helps a patient's muscles, bones, and joints recover after a serious illness, injury, or operation. She or he uses a range of techniques, such as exercise, massage, heat, and electrical treatment.

What does an occupational therapist do?

An occupational therapist helps to stimulate and develop a person's physical and mental skills after a long illness, or if they have a disability of some kind.

What is a pediatrician?

A pediatrician is a doctor who specializes in the treatment and care of children.

What is cosmetic surgery?

Cosmetic surgery is an operation carried out solely to improve the appearance of a person.

What causes a headache?

A headache is usually caused by tension or pressure in the head or neck. There are many possible causes such as poor posture, fatigue, anxiety, or infection.

What is a migraine?

A migraine is a severe headache accompanied by disturbed vision, such as spots before the eyes, and sometimes an upset stomach. Migraines may run in families. There is no single cause.

What is tennis elbow?

Tennis elbow is pain, stiffness, and swelling at the elbow. It is not just caused by tennis—any excessive use of the elbow joint can bring it on.

What is a prosthesis?

A prosthesis is an artificial replacement for a part of the body. An artificial leg, a glass eye, and an artificial heart valve are all examples.

What is cancer?

Cancer is the uncontrolled division and spread of rogue cells, which may destroy healthy cells. There are many forms of cancer, and some are treatable.

What is dental amalgam?

Amalgam is a material used to fill teeth. It consists of an alloy of mercury with other metals. When it sets, it is very durable.

What is an antidote?

An antidote is a substance that neutralizes or counteracts the effects of a poison.

What would an astringent do to you?

An astringent is a substance that dries out tissue, particularly skin. Astringents are used in skin treatments and antiperspirants.

What do psychologists study?

Psychologists study the human mind—thought, perception, emotion, behavior, and learning.

What is clergyman's knee?

Clergyman's knee is swelling just below the knee, caused by kneeling for long periods.

What is trigger finger?

Trigger finger is when a finger becomes locked in a tightly bent position because inflamed tissue has trapped tendons in it.

What is *déjà vu*?

Déjà vu is French for "already seen." It is the sense of having experienced something before, even though it is a new experience.

What is ECT?

ECT, short for electroconvulsive therapy, is a type of electric shock treatment given to some people suffering from serious depression.

What are fallen arches?

Fallen arches occur when someone becomes flat-footed because the muscles or ligaments in the arches of their feet have suddenly weakened.

What is a blue baby?

A blue baby is one that is born lacking a normal supply of oxygen. Its blood is therefore blue, making the baby appear bluish.

What is a frozen shoulder?

A frozen shoulder is stiffness and pain in the shoulder that makes normal movement impossible.

What are surfer's nodules?

These are bony growths surfers may get on the knees from kneeling on surfboards.

What causes whiplash?

Whiplash may be caused by car accidents if someone's neck is wrenched violently back and forth. This damages the spinal cord.

What is a hernia?

A hernia is the displacement of a part of the body. The most common type of hernia is where part of the intestine bulges through the wall of the abdomen.

WHERE?

Where did human beings come from?

Many scientists believe that the first true humans came into being about 100,000 years ago. They are believed to have evolved, through a number of stages, from an ape-like creature called *Australopithecus*, which lived in Africa four million years ago.

Where is your third eye?

The "third eye" is your pineal gland, a small structure deep within the brain. It receives information from your eyes, and its activity is influenced by the amount of daylight.

Where are your gingiva?

Gingiva is the Latin name for the gums surrounding the base of your teeth.

Where do people get growing pains?

Growing pains are aches and pains in the limbs, most common in children age 6 to 12.

Where is the jejunum?

The jejunum is one of the three parts of the small intestine. It comes between the duodenum and the ileum.

Where are mechanical receptors found?

Mechanical receptors are found in muscles, tendons, and ligaments. They are nerve cells that send messages to your brain when your joints are bent and your muscles are stretched. This means that you always know the position of your arms and legs without having to look at them.

Where are your adenoids?

The adenoids are fleshy pads of tissue at the back of the nose above the palate. Like the tonsils, the adenoids fight infection.

Where does a callus develop?

Calluses (areas of thick, protective skin) are most common on the hands and feet, but grow on any area subjected to continued pressure.

Where is your body clock?

You have more than one body clock, but one of the most important is in the pineal gland in your brain. It helps regulate your 24-hour cycles, such as your sleep-activity cycle.

Where does the term "long in the tooth" come from?

As people reach middle age, gum disease may cause their gums to shrink, making the teeth look longer. This gave rise to the saying "long in the tooth" to denote an older person.

Where are the saccule and utricle?

The saccule and utricle are two fluid-filled swellings in the inner ear. They detect the position of your head relative to the pull of gravity.

Where is your buccal cavity?

The buccal cavity is another name for the inside of your mouth.

Where are your carotid arteries?

The carotid arteries run through the neck to carry blood to the head.

Where would you find a sinew?

Joined to a muscle. A sinew is another name for a tendon (the tissue attaching muscle to bone).

Where are your coronary arteries?

The coronary arteries form a network over the surface of the heart, bringing the heart its own blood supply, food, and oxygen.

Where are your eyeteeth?

Your eyeteeth, or canines, are the sharp, pointed teeth just behind your front teeth.

Where did Legionnaire's disease get its name?

Legionnaire's disease is a type of pneumonia that got its name from the occasion when the disease was first identified clearly. This was at an American Legion convention in 1976.

Where are your humors?

The humors are found in your eye. The aqueous humor is the clear liquid in the front of your eye, while the vitreous humor is the clear jelly at the back.

Where are your hamstrings?

The hamstrings are the tendons that connect the hamstring muscles at the back of your thigh with your lower leg bones. Injuries to hamstring muscles are fairly common in athletes.

Where would you find the jugular?

Deep in the neck. There are four jugular veins carrying blood from the head back to the heart.

Where would you find an incompetent aorta?

In the heart. "Incompetent aorta" is the technical name for an aortic valve that does not work properly. As a result, blood leaks from the aorta, the main artery, back into the heart.

Where does lanugo appear?

Lanugo appears on the head of a human fetus. It is the first downy hair that develops at 3 to 5 months, and is normally shed at 7 to 8 months.

Where is the uvula?

The uvula is the floppy piece of tissue dangling down in the middle of your throat. Nobody knows what it is for.

Where would you find a lumen?

A lumen is the hollow space within a tube. For example, the hole running through a blood vessel is called the lumen.

Where are the orbits?

The orbits are in your skull. They are the sockets that contain your eyeballs.

Where would you find your pacemaker?

Your pacemaker is in the wall of the right atrium of your heart. It controls your heartbeat. If it is faulty, an artificial pacemaker can be inserted.

Where are your basal ganglia?

The basal ganglia are paired clusters of nerve cells in the base of the brain. They help control your body movements to make them smooth.

Where is your pharynx?

The pharynx is the technical name for your throat—the passage that leads from the back of your mouth and nose to your windpipe and esophagus.

Where would you find vernix?

Vernix is the white, greasy substance that coats the skin of a newborn baby.

Where would you find calculus?

You might find calculus in the kidneys or gallbladder. Calculus is a deposit or hard mass of crystal that forms kidney stones and gall stones. It may also form a coating on teeth.

Where would you find your coccyx?

Your coccyx is at the base of the spine. It is made up of four small vertebrae that are fused together.

Where is your dorsal side?

This is the back of your body—technically, the uppermost side of your body when you are lying face down. Your front is called the ventral side.

Where is the tarsus?

The tarsus is the ankle. It contains seven different bones altogether.

Where would you find a ligature?

You would find a ligature at the site of an injury or wound during surgery. It is a length of thread used for tying off a blood vessel or other tube to prevent it from leaking.

Where do you find mesentery?

Mesentery is the name of the transparent membrane that attaches various organs to the inside wall of your abdomen. The mesentery keeps your "innards" from moving around.

Where is your umbilicus?

Your umbilicus is on your stomach—umbilicus is the medical name for your belly button, or navel.

Where is the palate?

Your palate is the roof of the mouth. It separates the mouth from the nasal cavity. It is hard at the front and soft at the back.

Where is your spleen?

Your spleen is a long thin organ in the top left of your abdomen. It removes and destroys worn-out red blood cells and produces white blood cells that help fight infection.

Where was the first case of influenza?

Influenza was first recorded in Paris in 1414, but there may have been cases before this date.

Where does a tapeworm live?

A tapeworm lives in the intestines of its host (this is sometimes a human), where it absorbs food through its body wall. A person may be infected with a tapeworm by eating poorly cooked meat.

Where are the crypts of Lieberkühn?

The crypts of Lieberkühn are tiny digestive glands found in the wall of the small intestine. They produce digestive enzymes that are released into the intestines to break down food.

Where is the metacarpus?

The metacarpus is the name given to the bones of the middle of the hand, between the wrist and the fingers.

Where would you find the bony labyrinth?

The bony labyrinth is a series of connected cavities that you would find in the inner ear. It is involved in both hearing and keeping your balance.

Where were false teeth first worn?

In 700 B.C. the ancient Etruscans, in Italy, were wearing false teeth made from bone or ivory.

Where did early anatomists find corpses to study?

Until the seventeenth century, it was forbidden in Europe to cut up human bodies for scientific purposes. Early anatomists would therefore dig up graves illegally to get bodies for research.

Where were the first cataract operations performed?

In India in 500 B.C., a doctor named Susrata performed the first operation to remove a cataract and restore a patient's sight.

Where is the pyloric sphincter?

The pyloric sphincter is between the stomach and the small intestine. It is a ring of muscle that acts as a valve. When it relaxes, food enters the small intestine from the stomach.

Where would you get a goiter?

A goiter is a large swelling on the neck. It is caused by the enlargement of the thyroid gland due to a lack of iodine. Goiters are more common in mountainous areas where there is no natural iodine in the drinking water.

Where was the Red Cross established?

The International Red Cross was established in Geneva, Switzerland, in 1863.

WHEN?

When were microbes discovered?

The first microbes were discovered in 1762, by an Austrian doctor, M. A. Plenciz. Most of the microbes that we know about today were discovered by the end of the nineteenth century.

When was the first blood transfusion carried out?

In the seventeenth century, unsuccessful transfusions were carried out between animals and humans. The first blood transfusions using human blood were carried out in 1818.

When was the first artificial heart used?

The first artificial heart was implanted in 1982. Artificial hearts were used, not very successfully, as a short-term measure for those waiting for a heart transplant.

When was the first artificial pacemaker fitted?

The first artificial pacemaker (used to stimulate the heart to beat) was invented by Dr. Ake Senning of Sweden in 1958. The first working models were implanted in patients' chests in the early 1960s.

When did vacuum cleaners help save lives?

In 1927, Philip Drinken of Harvard University developed the first iron lung. His first model incorporated two vacuum cleaners. Later versions of the iron lung were used to keep alive patients whose breathing muscles had been paralyzed by polio.

When was drilling a hole in the head a form of treatment?

Trepanning (drilling or removing part of the skull) was practiced in Neolithic times (5000 to 2500 B.C.). A few people survived this treatment—some of the skulls show signs of healing.

When would you have a barium meal?

You would have a barium meal if a doctor suspected there was something wrong with your intestines. X rays cannot penetrate barium, so the intestines show up as a clear outline on an X-ray picture.

When were bone fractures first treated?

In ancient Egypt, in about 3000 B.C., Athotis recommended the use of cloth soaked in mud and then dried as a means of supporting fractured bones.

When were ambulances first used?

The first ambulances were horse-drawn wagons used in war—the Spanish army carried wounded soldiers from battle in the Siege of Malaga in 1487. The first civilian ambulances were introduced in New York City in 1869.

When did the paramedic service begin?

The paramedic service was introduced in the mid-1960s, in the United States. Paramedics are highly trained medical staff who give patients vital emergency treatment before they reach a hospital.

When was bloodletting used as a treatment?

Bloodletting—bleeding a patient by a cut or using blood-sucking worms called leeches—was used up until the eighteenth century as a treatment for almost any ailment.

When were eyeglasses invented?

No one is sure when eyeglasses first appeared; we know that Europeans were wearing them in the thirteenth century. The Italian traveler Marco Polo reported that he saw people in eyeglasses in China in 1275.

When is a cell a zygote?

When it is the first cell of an embryo. The zygote is the cell formed when a sperm from the father fertilizes an egg from the mother.

When was the first appendix removed successfully?

Surprisingly, as long ago as 1735, Claudius Aymand, an English military surgeon, successfully removed a patient's appendix.

When are very cold temperatures used in surgery?

Temperatures as low as –256°F are used in some eye operations and to remove cancers and birthmarks, since they can destroy tissue with little scarring. The metal instruments used are cooled in liquid nitrogen.

When do you swallow a bolus?

You swallow a bolus every time you eat. Food is shaped by the tongue and teeth into a ball, or bolus, since this is easier for us to swallow.

When is something intravenous?

When it is in a vein. For example, an injection is intravenous when the end of the needle is inserted into a vein.

When is something *in vivo*?

When it is inside the body. An *in vivo* examination is when a disease is examined within a patient's body. If the disease is studied by observing the disease microbes in a test tube, then it is *in vitro* (meaning "in glassware").

When does a knee lock?

A knee locks—so that it is unable to move backward or forward—when the cartilage tears and pieces get into the knee joint.

When was the first filling?

Records show that tooth filling was carried out in ancient Sumer (modern Iraq) around the year 3000 B.C.

When was Bedlam opened?

Bedlam, the first mental hospital in Europe, was opened in London in the fourteenth century.

When was the first medical school founded?

A medical school was founded at Salerno in Italy in the tenth century. It was the major center of medical learning in Europe for 200 years.

When was tobacco used as a medicine?

Native Americans were using tobacco as a medicine when Christopher Columbus reached America in 1492. After the plant was brought back to Europe, tobacco was grown as a medicine to help people relax.

When were contact lenses introduced?

Contact lenses were first introduced in 1958.

When were the first glass eyes made?

Glass eyes were first made around 1579.

When might you perform Valsalva's maneuver?

You do this when you are about to sneeze. It is when you try to breathe out while your nasal passage is closed.

When do people get lockjaw?

People get lockjaw if they have a tetanus infection. Lockjaw is a painful spasm of the jaw muscles that makes it difficult or impossible to open the mouth.

When does looking to one side of an object allow you to see it better?

Looking slightly to one side of an object allows you to see it more clearly in dim light. This is because the light-sensitive cells at the sides of your eye (the rods) are more sensitive to the amount of light present than those in the center (the cones).

When was the first transplant carried out?

In the seventeenth century, the first skin grafts (skin tissue transplants) were performed by the Boiani family of Italy. The method they used is still practiced today.

WHY?

Why are we sometimes nauseous?

We are sometimes nauseous if we eat too much or if food or drink irritates the lining of the stomach. Being nauseous is a useful way to stop us from becoming ill from what we eat.

Why would a doctor hit you with a hammer?

Your doctor might hit you with a rubber hammer if he or she were testing your reflexes. You would cross one leg over the other, and the doctor would tap you just below the kneecap with the hammer. Your leg should jerk upward if your reflexes are working properly.

Why are people so different?

At least 10,000 genes give us our characteristics. Scientists calculate that it is practically impossible for any two people to receive exactly the same genetic information—except, of course, identical twins.

Why is the first year of life so important?

The first year of life is so important because it is the time when considerable growth and development take place. For example, many inter-connections between the brain cells are laid down during the first year. The right care is vital to stimulate the baby's development.

Why is childplay so important?

Through their play children learn how to coordinate their movements, how to explore their surroundings, and how to get along with other people.

Why does hair sometimes suddenly go gray?

If a person has an illness or emotional shock he may lose some of his hair. Darker hairs are lost more readily than light ones, so the remaining hair is lighter. This may happen in a few days or weeks.

Why is there a red-and-white pole outside a barber's shop?

The white stands for bandages and the red for blood. Before 1800, a lot of surgery, such as tooth extractions, was carried out by untrained barber-surgeons.

Why were World War II pilots asked not to eat beans?

Pilots were asked to avoid eating beans because they produce gases in the digestive system. There was concern that when the pilots reached high altitudes, the gases would expand and cause pain which would distract the pilots.

Why are lips red?

Lips are red because the skin there is very thin, and there is a rich supply of blood vessels just below the surface. The color outlines the mouth clearly so that changes in expression are easily seen.

Why can scratching relieve an itch?

Scratching overwhelms the delicate, irritating sensation of itching with a much more powerful one. Scratching can also release natural pain-killers called endorphins.

Why can I make my eyes turn inward, but not outward?

We need to make our eyes turn inward so that we can focus on close objects. We do not need to make our eyes turn outward. If we did, each eye would have a completely separate view of our surroundings.

Why does a doctor tap a patient's chest?

By listening to the sound produced when he or she taps a patient's chest, a doctor can tell if the patient has certain kinds of lung ailments.

Why is it best to exercise little and often?

You will become much more fit if you exercise three or four times a week for 20 minutes than if you exercise only once a week for an hour.

Why do men have nipples?

Nobody knows. Nipples form early in a fetus's development, and in a female they form part of the woman's breasts, which produce milk to feed her babies. In men, however, the nipples do not seem to have a specific function.

Why do I sometimes get a lump in my throat?

It feels like a lump, but it is actually a tightening of muscles in the throat. It seems to be a side effect of the hormone adrenaline, which may be released when we are anxious or sad.

Why are additives put in foods?

Additives are put in foods to improve their appearance, taste, and texture, or to make them last longer on the shelf.

Why do I get circles under my eyes when I am tired?

The skin around the eye is thin, with a rich blood supply. When we are tired or ill, the blood supply to this area increases, and it appears as puffiness and small circles.

Why do children get so many diseases?

Children catch many diseases because they have not developed immunity to them. By the time we are adults, we have already had many of these diseases and developed immunity to them so that we do not catch them again.

Why do some people have a lisp?

A lisp is a mild speech problem in which the tongue pokes between the teeth so that the person makes a "th" sound when he is trying to say "ss." This may be because the teeth are a little out of shape. This can be corrected. Many small children who have lost their front teeth speak with a lisp.

Why do we have a navel?

The navel is a scar showing where our umbilical cord was attached.

Why do people get a tetanus shot after an accident?

Tetanus is a bacterial disease that can enter the body through wounds. A tetanus shot contains antibodies to prevent the disease.

Why do people get ingrown toenails?

Ingrown toenails are caused by tight-fitting shoes, poor personal hygiene, or not cutting toenails straight across. The nail grows into the skin at either side of the toe.

Why are snakes linked with medicine?

In several ancient civilizations snakes were believed to have magical healing properties. Priests traveled with containers of harmless snakes, which were believed to lick the wounds of the sick and injured.

Why do I sometimes twitch as I fall asleep?

When we sink into a deep sleep there is sometimes an upsurge in brain activity. This sends out electrical signals to the muscles, making them contract in a sharp spasm.

Why can cooking food destroy its "goodness"?

Cooking can destroy some of the vitamins in food. For example, vitamin C in vegetables is broken down by prolonged boiling and is lost in the cooking water.

Why are astronauts taller in space than on Earth?

In space there is no gravity, so the astronauts' bones can spread apart a little at the joints, making them as much as half an inch taller.

Why are some medicines injected?

If some medicines are swallowed, they are either broken down by enzymes in the stomach or they cannot get across the intestinal wall. To work, they must be injected directly into a tissue or organ. An injection also gets the medicine circulating in the bloodstream much faster.

HOW?

How fast can we run?

The fastest sprinters reach speeds of about 27 miles an hour over short distances.

How long can people live?

In countries where there is good medical care, men can expect to live an average of 70 years, and women, 75 years.

How many sweat glands do you have?

You have about 3 million sweat glands in your skin. If they were stretched out and laid end to end they would cover about 30 miles.

How much does the liver weigh?

The liver weighs about 4.5 pounds and is the heaviest organ in the body, apart from the skin.

How many muscles do we use to walk?

We use more than 200 different muscles when we walk. Our leg muscles are some of the biggest and strongest in our bodies.

How many ribs do we have?

Most people have 24 ribs, 12 on each side.

How many red blood cells die every second?

About 2.5 million red blood cells die every second, but they are replaced just as quickly.

How many bones does a newborn baby have?

A newborn baby has 305 bones, about 100 more than an adult. However, some of these bones fuse together as the baby grows older.

How long is the spinal cord?

On average, the spinal cord of an adult is 17 inches long.

How many eggs does a woman produce in her life?

Most women release one ripe egg every month, over about 35 years. That adds up to over 400 eggs. A woman's ovaries contain thousands of unripe eggs that never develop.

How much saliva do you produce in a day?

Adults produce up to 1.5 quarts of saliva a day.

How can you tell if you have broken a bone?

Unless the bone is sticking out at a strange angle it is difficult to tell if it is broken. The pain, swelling, and bruising could be due to a strained joint.

How can we hear our name mentioned across a noisy room?

We can pick out our name from the background noise because we have selective attention—our brain can select things that are important to us and tune out those that are not.

How does a boxer become punch-drunk?

Physical blows to the head can shake the brain and kill nerve cells. Boxers may sustain so many blows that they can cause slow thinking and slurred speech, as if the boxer were drunk.

How did the Achilles tendon get its name?

The Achilles tendon is at the back of the heel. It is named after the ancient Greek hero Achilles, who was invulnerable—except for his heel.

How did the atlas vertebra get its name?

The atlas is the topmost vertebra in the spine. It supports the heavy weight of the head. It is named after Atlas, a character from Greek mythology. He was punished by the gods and forced to hold up the pillars separating Heaven from Earth.

How much of your brain is water?

Your brain is about 80 percent water.

How do you meditate?

A person meditates by calming her mind and clearing it of everyday thoughts. This is usually achieved by concentrating on breathing patterns or quietly repeating a simple phrase.

How much water do you lose in a day?

An adult loses 1.5 to 2 quarts of water a day. About half of this is in urine, and the rest is mostly in exhaled breath and sweat.

How is AIDS transmitted?

HIV, the virus that is believed to cause AIDS, can be passed on through sexual intercourse with an infected person, or by sharing a needle used by an infected person. If a mother has HIV, her baby will probably be born with HIV.

How can a doctor tell if someone is really dead?

A doctor looks for vital signs—a pulse, evidence of breathing, and a narrowing of the pupil when a bright light is shined into the eye. If these key signs are absent, the person is certified dead.

How powerful is a microscope?

A standard light microscope can magnify an image up to about 1,500 times. An electron microscope can magnify up to about 500,000 times.

How much iron does the body contain?

The average adult's body contains enough iron to make a nail 1 inch long.

How does a doctor use a bronchoscope?

A bronchoscope is a special type of endoscope, or flexible viewing cable. It is inserted through a patient's mouth and is used to examine the air passages leading to the lungs.

How dangerous is a wart?

Most warts are completely harmless and disappear on their own in time.

How quickly do nerve cells multiply?

Before birth, nerve cells in a fetus's brain form at the rate of 250,000 a minute. After birth, the production of new cells slows down right away.

How quickly do nerve cells die?

After the age of 20, about 10,000 nerve cells in the brain die each day and are not replaced.

How did altitude affect the 1968 Olympics?

In 1968 the Olympic Games were held in Mexico City, at an altitude of over a mile above sea level. As a result, all the medal winners in the long-distance events were athletes who had gotten used to high altitudes.

How many people are there in the world?

There are over 5 billion people living on Earth.

How fast is the world population increasing?

The world population is increasing at the rate of about 200,000 people a day. At this rate, the population will double in less than 70 years.

How many times does your heart beat in a lifetime?

At an average of 75 beats a minute over 70 years, the heart will beat over 2.75 billion times.

How serious is frostbite?

Frostbite—damage to tissues caused by extreme cold—can be very serious, since the damaged tissues may die and need to be removed.

How good is our sense of smell?

Our noses can detect a chemical that has a concentration of only 4 parts per million when it is almost 4 miles away. But our sense of smell is weak compared to that of other mammals.

How much liquid do we drink in a lifetime?

In an average lifetime, we drink about 51,000 quarts of liquid.

Index

Page numbers in *italic*
refer to illustrations.

ACKNOWLEDGMENTS

The publishers wish to thank the following artists for contributing to this book:

Craig Austin; Marion Appleton; Kuo Kang Chen; Richard Coombes; Mark Franklin; Ray Grinaway; Ron Jobson (Kathy Jakeman); Roger Kent (Garden Studios); Mike Lacey (Simon Girling Associates); Mainline Design; Maltings Partnership; Janos Marffy (Kathy Jakeman); The McRae Agency; Paul Richardson; Bernard Robinson; Eric Robson (Garden Studios); Mike Saunders (Kathy Jakeman); Rob Shone; Mark Stacey; Roger Stewart; Lucy Su; Linda Thursby; Kevin Toy (Garden Studios); Phil Weare.

Reference for the iron lung illustration on page 22 kindly supplied by Stan Hood of DMB TOOLS.

The publishers wish to thank the following for supplying photographs for this book:

Page 7 Science Photo Library (S.P.L.); 13 Rex Features; 21 S.P.L; 23 S.P.L; 24 Mark Shearman; 31 S.P.L; 32 Popperfoto; 35 National Medical Slide Bank; 45 John Walmsley; 59 S.P.L; 63 Institute of Laryngology and Otology; 71 S.P.L; 77 ZEFA; 79 Rex Features; 81 S.P.L; 85 S.P.L; 91 David Simson; 96 ZEFA; 103 Mansell Collection; 105 Allsport; 108 S.P.L.

Picture Research: Elaine Willis